PLEASURE MODEL

PLEASURE MODEL

NETHERWORLD

BOOK 1

CHRISTOPHER ROWLEY

A TOM DOHERTY ASSOCIATES BOOK
NEW YORK

HEAVY METAL PULP: PLEASURE MODEL: NETHERWORLD BOOK ONE

A Tor Book
Published by Tom Doherty Associates, LLC
175 Fifth Avenue
New York, NY 10010

www.tor-forge.com

Design by Greg Collins

Tor® is a registered trademark of Tom Doherty Associates, LLC.

Library of Congress Cataloging-in-Publication Data

Rowley, Christopher, 1948–
    Heavy metal pulp : pleasure model / Christopher Rowley. — 1st ed.
        p. cm. — (Netherworld ; book 1)
    "A Tom Doherty Associates book."
    ISBN 978-0-7653-2388-0
    1. Murder—Investigation—Fiction.   I. Title.   II. Title: pleasure model.
    PS3568.O9368H43 2010
    813'.54—dc22

                                                    2009041229

First Edition: February 2010

Printed in the United States of America

0 9 8 7 6 5 4 3 2 1

PLEASURE MODEL

CHAPTER 1

The man was a massive specimen. Heavy shoulders, powerful arms, solid delts and lats. The deeply lined face was hidden in shadows, the head bowed with pain, but it was a strong face, brutal even, or so Mistress Julia thought.

She had finished. One hundred strokes with the single-tail whip, following on eighty with the number three rattan cane. All delivered quite slowly, ten seconds apart, stretching the ordeal out to an hour. Blood ran from several welts on his back and buttocks. His head, shaved to the skin, glistened with sweat.

He dropped to his knees and kissed the feet of the

Virgin Mary. The statue stood, smiling serenely in the living room. Blood smeared the polished marble floor as he swayed.

He was mumbling, as he always did. She heard the words, though she scarcely understood them.

> *Bruised, derided, cursed, defiled,*
> *please behold your evil child*
> *all with bloody scourges rent;*
> *For the sins upon his nation*
> *save him from the desolation*
> *that awaits him down in hell.*

Mistress Julia kept her distance. Clients usually groveled before she beat them. With her ash blond hair slicked back in a ponytail, she was dressed in her most "severe" mode, black patent leather bodysuit, high boots with four-inch heels, gloves, and mask. But this client was never actually involved in a sexual scene. Other than kissing her boots and begging for the whip, he asked for nothing that was normally part of her practice. This one just wanted to be punished.

And punished severely.

She had never beaten a man who simply took it the way this one did. Never a murmur, a groan, a cry, a tear, nothing, until she was done and he fell down before the six-foot marble statue and wept as he mumbled his prayers.

She turned on her heel and stalked away. Whatever Mr. Sangacha's problem was, she had done her part. Another four hundred New Dollars waited in the envelope on the glass table. She picked it up as she headed for the bathroom.

Prostrate before thee, I make this humble act of reparation
for the outrages which thou hast received from me. . . .

He was still praying, the fervor thick in his throat, as she closed the bathroom door.

Mistress Julia—real name Angela Bricken—normally worked with her clients at her specially equipped basement dungeon in a nice modern house over in Ramapo. However, Sangacha had insisted from the beginning

on being visited in his own home. It was not her favorite mode of operation. In the dungeon she had her security set up, with various technologies that could rapidly immobilize a man if he turned violent during a session.

But Sangacha had never given her the slightest trouble. He never deviated from the scene and he always paid in full, on time and without complaint.

The one problem, of course, was the surveillance. Cams were everywhere, and for her own good reasons Angie Bricken didn't care to be lensed too often in any one place. So she had to take precautions.

She rinsed off the whip and the cane as she got the hot water running, then peeled off her boots and unzipped her suit. Some clients begged for these tasks, and some were rewarded with them, and other things too, but only after they'd paid their dues. Mistress Julia had learned a lot of things about men over the years.

Whip, boots, and suit went into her bag as she stripped down. For a moment she looked at herself in the floor-to-ceiling mirror. Still desirable, she thought, even at fifty. Intensive antioxidant treatments, strict diet, and rigorous exercise were partly responsible. Her extended medical program with monthly checkups and prevention-interventions took care of the rest. Only the most careful examination of her face could reveal that she was anything but a day over thirty.

The shower was good. Sangacha had a real high-tech unit, with jets at three levels that pulsed on a cycle of different frequencies. She enjoyed the hard-driving

water, surrendering to the heat, feeling cleaner by the second.

Angie never scheduled anything else on Sangacha days. She realized she was hungry, so she broke out of the Julia construct and pressed a fingertip to her right ear, where her phone chip was lodged.

"That organic place, down in Tarrytown. Book me in for lunch."

A massive thud shook the shower.

"What the fuck?" She turned off the water and pulled back the curtain, which probably saved her life. The next blast was unmistakable—shotgun. A scream followed, and cursing, and then a rapid thud-thud-thud that she knew had to be some kind of automatic weapon equipped with a silencer.

For a moment she stood frozen, terrified and astonished. Then the shotgun went off again and something or somebody slammed into the bathroom door.

That got her moving. She swept her bag off the floor, stuffed it into the dirty towel bin. It fit, just, and she shut the lid. Then she spun around and switched off the lights. Rubbing the foot towel over the floor to mop up the drips, she yanked open the door to the cabinet under the sink.

A tight fit, but she could do it. She had to do it. She was certain of that, if she wanted to live.

There were some more thud-thuds, and a lot of loud cursing. A man was whimpering in pain.

She scrunched her body down under the sink, got her legs up into the space on the other side of the pipes, pulled her head inside, stuffed the foot towel under her ass, which helped to cushion her hip against the metal drain, and tugged the door shut. It did so with a plastic click that left her briefly wondering if she could open it again from inside, or if she'd be stuck there until who knew when.

Which was fucking absurd, because whatever was going on out there in the duplex, it involved guns and that meant only one thing: death.

She waited, shivering, fear coiling inside her like a cold dark creature.

The last twenty-five years had been like this, since the day she'd gotten the personality modification program and become Mistress Julia. One minute she was a dominatrix, afraid of nothing, in command, and the next she was helpless little Angie, drowning in her own fear, praying for Julia to save her.

"You stupid fuck!" There came a loud moan of pain and, she imagined, the sound of something or someone being dragged.

There was a crash, then silence.

Her mind ran wildly though scenarios. She didn't know who Sangacha was. As was often the case in her business, she didn't want to know that kind of thing.

Was it a mob hit? Was he some kind of crim? She had wondered about that. His habit of praying for forgiveness when she'd laid into him had the sound of a man who'd done terrible things in his life.

Then she heard the door to the bathroom open and a heavy tread on the tile floor.

"Where the fuck is she?" asked a male voice.

"Must've gotten out just before we arrived," said another.

"Check the parking. Hurry."

Boots retreated. She stayed where she was, the fear now like a sword of ice running up her guts. The bathroom door slammed.

What the fuck was going on?

The footsteps had ceased. Still she waited. Had they gone? Were they playing games? She kept as still as she

possibly could, though the difficulties of her confinement were now making themselves apparent. Something was digging into the small of her back, and her head was crushed in between the side of the sink and the side of the cabinet.

She wanted to get to her car and put as many miles as she could between herself and this complex as quickly as possible. She'd go straight up to the woods and hide out. Up there she was somebody else, a whole other ID.

She was about to open the door when she heard a sudden rush of footsteps go by. Then the bathroom door banged open and the light went on, sending a gleam through the crack at the edge of the door to her hiding place.

"She ain't here," a voice groaned. "I'm fucking bleeding!"

"Here's a towel," drawled another. "Try not to bleed all over the truck."

Footsteps retreated, another door slammed, and every-thing was quiet again.

Fuck indeed. Fuck, fuck, fuck, she'd almost gotten her-self caught there.

She waited.

Time passed. The thing digging into her back turned into torture. Angie tried not to let it all get to her. She had to stay calm. But Mistress Julia had other ideas.

Take a rest, Angie. Take your nerves and your weak-nesses and your hunger for a piece of dark chocolate and shut the fuck up. It's time for iron control. Time to stay alive.

Julia took back the reins with the familiar sliding sen-sation. The dominatrix persona started her life on an A2 chip that Angie plugged in and out of the microsocket behind her right ear. At first, Angie had been terrified of Julia, afraid one day she would completely dominate her life. But Angie had learned the hard way—she needed Julia. Now, the stern alpha female was always there, wait-ing just below the surface. Angie didn't even need the plug-in anymore.

Minutes crawled by. Julia counted seconds like whip strokes. When the count reached a hundred she pushed hard. The door popped open with a bang and she fell out onto the bathroom floor.

Right before her eyes were huge, bloody boot prints, leading in and out of the bathroom.

She pulled her bag out of the towel bin and hurriedly got into her Zipdex bodysuit. Now she pulled out two face-cloths and wiped everything she might have touched with her bare skin, working quickly and, she prayed, effectively. She mopped out the shower, did her best on the curtain, and ran some more water to be sure while she worked on the space under the sink. Everything went into her bag.

Done, she slung her bag over her shoulder and padded into the hall. Bullet holes riddled the wall. It looked as if someone had tried to mop up a quart of blood, and hadn't

done a very good job. She went the other way, through the kitchen, and came out in the dining area. Another couple of steps and she saw him.

Sangacha lay on his back. There was a sawed-off shotgun lying close by. A pool of blood spread beneath him, washing over the feet of the Virgin Mary.

At the front door she put on her sneakers, her big mirrored sunglasses, and her pink and white Yankees cap with the bill pulled down low over her face. There wasn't time for makeup to disguise herself any further. Any images caught by the cams at this point were going to be studied intensively, she knew. She attached a little distortion box to the right side of her sunglasses frame. The box was expensive, and illegal, but it would blur her features, even her outline, to any ordinary camera.

Mistress Julia opened the door and peered both ways before bolting for the stairs. Because there'd been a work crew painting signage on the main parking, she'd gone around to the service worker area. It was smaller, even the

spaces were narrower, but she was very glad she'd used it since the killers wouldn't expect her to have parked there.

She cracked open the blue door to the parking and paused. Had they left someone here to take care of her, just in case? Working methodically, she looked down the aisles and into the corners.

With a deep breath, she headed for her car, prepared to run at the slightest sign of someone waiting for her. The car door opened for her and she slid inside.

"Ridgetop," she whispered, and the car slid out with the soft whine of the electric engine. She knew there were cameras at the exit ramp, so she kept her head down, letting just the pink Yankees cap be seen. A few moments later she was on the access road and the car began to accelerate. As she started to breathe normally again, questions and answers, most of them terrifying, boiled to the surface.

Shit. She really liked this town. But now she had to run again. There were some problems not even Mistress Julia could handle.

CHAPTER

Kingston, New York, had opened for business in the days of Charles II. Of course, hardly anyone who lived there now knew or cared about the town's history.

It was raining again, hard. Huge torrents of dirty water were sluicing down the drains with a familiar throbbing sound. The riffraff had long since been swept off the stretch of Broadway near the HudVal PD building.

Rook Venner, Senior Investigating Officer, Homicide, looked out the window of his office. For a moment he caught his reflection in the glass, dark hair cut short, broad forehead, prominent cheekbones. Thin lips twitched in a smile. Not too bad, he thought. He ought to be more successful with women than he was. It was the job, of course; it turned them off.

The implant in his right ear, the office phone, beeped once.

"What've we got?"

"One-eight-seven," his partner reported. "In an upscale devo down by Peekskill."

"Our side of the line?"

"Apparently."

Pity about that. South of Front Street and it was Westchester's problem, not his.

Rook began assembling his kit. Since this wasn't a mission to the uninsured world, he didn't need body armor, or the knock-hammer, or any of the heavy toys. He did pack his gun and helmet, or "technical headpiece," as the manual liked to call it.

His partner, Assistant Investigator Lindi MacEar—tall, blond, fond of triathlons—strode down the hall. She had all her gear strapped on: gun, lights, chem lab, specimen safe, multicam, the works, bar the armor and hand-to-hand weapons.

"Ready, boss?"

"Yeah." He pulled on his raincoat, flipped up the hood. "Unless we drown before we get to the damned car."

He checked his chest pocket for the reassuring solidity of Ingrid, his Nokia Supa. Way beyond regulation, of course, but when it came to encryption, the best handheld device you could get.

The gutters were overflowing at the back of the building, sending sheets of water straight down into the courtyard. They were soaked by the time they got into the Nat 200. On the upside, traffic was light. Only idiots and cops drove in the summer monsoons. Rook let the car drive itself.

On the Thruway they rode the rail on the outside lane. The inside truck traffic howled past in its robotic way, exploding through the rain at more than two hundred miles an hour.

Seventeen minutes to the second from Kingston and they rolled up to the faux concrete portico of the development in Peekskill. Flashing lights and a swarm of cops in full combat gear were there to greet him. As he stepped out, a patrol officer saw the badge on his helmet and moved aside.

Two cops in tac-squad shells were positioned to cover the hallway down to the elevators. Upstairs, orange laser baffles blocked off the corridor, with another tac-suit to keep the curious away.

No sign of forced entry, Rook thought, glancing at the high-tech security locks.

Inside the apartment, the South Valley CSI team was already hard at work.

"Crazy shit," murmured Chatt Fletcher, a rotund, cheerful kid out of Brooklyn. He pointed to the blood spray on the walls and marble tiles. "Shotgun, heavy gauge. Fired three times, at least one hit."

"That's a lot of blood."

"Not the target. He's over there." Chatt looked over his shoulder into the high-ceilinged living room.

Rook observed a big man, naked, lying facedown beside a life-size marble statue of the Virgin Mary.

"Didn't help him much, did she," muttered Rook.

"Not a believer, boss?"

"Jury's out on that one." Rook patted his holster. "For now I'll keep some insurance."

Chatt read off his notes. "Vic is Manuel Sangacha, age sixty-seven, no known relatives. Nothing stolen."

"You left out an important detail," announced MacEar, checking her handheld. "This is General Manuel Sangacha."

"General?" Rook didn't like the sound of that.

"Retired in 'fifty-two. Service period began in 2019. Commanded a border division during the Emergency."

Rook chewed his lip. This sounded like stuff he didn't want to have anything to do with.

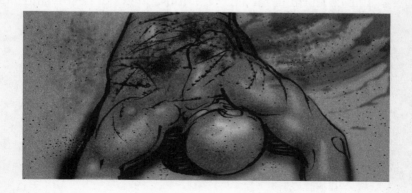

He tapped the button on his phone.

"Leave a message," said the chief's personal unit.

He did. Military stuff was dangerous. With luck the chief would pull him off this thing and call in military intelligence. Let them take care of their own.

Rook went back to business. "What's all that secondary damage?"

Chatt shrugged. "Back, buttocks, and thighs are covered in welts. Blows from a whip and something else, maybe a cane?"

Rook raised an eyebrow. "Hmm. Punishment or interrogation?"

"No idea. He's been dead about four hours."

"Messy. Murder weapon?"

"Early for forensics, but most likely a five-point-five millimeter. Sophisticated shit, delayed explosive rounds."

The usual thing for assassinations, quiet but deadly and small enough to be concealed from the sec cams. This was looking more and more like a corporate hit.

"What do we know from the security cams?"

"System was dazzled for about ninety minutes. Started at four o'clock, stopped at five-twenty-six."

"Lins, you want to try some of your magic?"

"On it, boss." Lindi tapped her handheld. "Chatt, feed me the sec cam footage."

Venner stalked slowly around the apartment. He had handled maybe a dozen corporate killings in his decade on Homicide. Usually the crime scene was so clean it squeaked. The killers were always ultraprofessional, left no traces, made no sound.

Then there was the whip. When hit teams had to extract info they usually used a combo of drugs to increase sensitivity and really painful tricks, like skinning a man's penis, or boiling his hands. These wounds weren't deep enough to cause that kind of pain. Chatt hadn't mentioned any fancy drug residues, though that might come with later analysis.

A straight-out corporate hit would seem the best fit here.

"One thing," Chatt mentioned. "Vic seems to have no chips, no active sub-cutes, no BIMS, not even an Insurance RFID."

"Well, he was military," Lindi said. "He had his removed when he got out."

"And never had others put in?"

Insured people wore a palette of implants, from uni-IDs to feelgoods and personality modules. Finding someone unchipped was freakish. No chips made Sangacha virtually invisible to sensors. What did the general have to hide?

"Here's something else interesting," Chatt reported. "Someone wiped the bathroom down."

Venner looked down the bloodstained hallway.

"No prints?"

"Lots of prints, but mostly Sangacha's. Same with DNA so far."

"The vic wet?"

"No, he's dry."

Rook studied the front door again. There were heavy-duty bolts top and bottom.

"Any sign of tampering?" Lindi asked without looking up from her handheld.

"Nope," said Chatt. "He either let them in or they had the code. He didn't have it bolted, either."

Just as likely, Sangacha felt like he ought to be safe and secure here, but another part of him said he wasn't. So he put on the bolts and bought the Remington six-shot. But he didn't lock the bolts, because it was a pain in the ass to have to unlock bolts to go in and out of your front door. But he did keep the Remington somewhere reasonably handy. Not good enough to save his life, but good enough to ruin someone else's day.

"Incoming call," the Nokia announced. "Chief Artoli."

"Thanks, Ingrid."

"Venner, what d'you got?" whispered a familiar voice in his right ear.

"The vic was a general. It's a corporate hit, but it's all wrong, blood everywhere."

"Keep this by the book, Detective. I don't want any of your shit," Area Chief Lisa Artoli ordered.

Venner and Chief Artoli went back a long way. Venner always got the job done but not without ruffling some feathers. Sometimes an entire goose.

"Shouldn't we hand this off to MI?" Rook asked.

"This is from Albany. Minimize cooperation with federal agencies."

"Christ." The state government was telling him to fuck the feds. "The feds are probably already on their way. This guy ran a border unit."

"Then do the dance. But if you get something good it goes to Albany and they make the decision."

"I hear you."

In other words, this was a political killing and Rook knew that meant extreme danger for everyone involved.

He turned back to MacEar. "Any luck with the cam footage?"

"Working on it."

"Come on, genius."

Lindi shot him a look.

A second later she displayed a grainy image from the parking lot cam. A blond woman in a pink baseball cap. It was a start.

"Woman left at five-oh-one, in the center of the dazzle."

Lindi was good. He probably didn't deserve her.

"Detective, we got something!" An officer came bounding into the apartment. "A witness, no, sorry—make that evidence."

Rook lifted an eyebrow. "You want to make up your mind?"

"Pleasure model. In a crate down in the storage unit."

"Christ." The vic hid a mod-bod so the neighbors wouldn't know how he got his kicks. "What kind?"

"Kind? Oh, it's a Pammy, I think."

"Ship it to the station and make sure none of your people get near it. I want whatever it knows unfiltered. Got it?"

"I've never seen one close up." Chatt grinned.

"What? A Pammy?" asked Lindi.

"Um, any pleasure model."

"Just keep your pants on," Lindi ordered with a half-smile.

Rook sighed. A mod-bod. These vat-grown gene humans had the IQ of a pocket watch and were completely illegal. Something else to make this case even weirder than it was—and a lot more difficult.

CHAPTER

"I am Plesur," whispered the creature, the thing, *it*. Though the longer he talked to her, or *it*, the harder it was to remember that this was not really a human being—or was it?

Of course, her—*its*—vocabulary was limited, but apart from that it was a gorgeous young woman, about twenty years old, with long golden hair, deep blue eyes, a pert little nose, and a large mouth loaded with heavy lips that worked like triggers on the heterosexual male mind.

Throw in perfect breasts, flat belly, firm ass, and long shapely legs and it was a composition in flesh designed for one purpose only, and designed terribly well.

"Plesur is the default name, just as it came out of the box," murmured Lindi from the other side of the room, where she was taking notes and running down leads on the 'net.

Plesur's blue eyes flicked back and forth between Rook and Lindi, filled with apprehension. Life had been turned upside down that day, evidenced in part by the fact that the mod was still wearing her black silk pajamas.

It certainly looked human. It had been born almost full grown in a laboratory, probably in the Philippines. It was smart enough to learn to speak, to perform simple

tasks, and do what it was designed to do—provide sexual pleasure to its owner. Of course it had no fertile eggs in its ovaries—these things could not breed. That would destroy their market value. Most mods had a life span of about ten years and could be purchased new for around N$400,000. Used models went for less, depending on how much time was left on their clocks.

They were illegal everywhere except China and Japan. Illegal or not, they were still common among the wealthy classes in every country. Pleasure models came in several different styles. Rook had seen dark-skinned types with gorgeous African features, and some exquisite Chinese varieties. But this one, the "Pammy," was the best known and the most popular in America.

Rook pointed to himself. "I am Venner. I ask you questions, okay?"

"Okay." The lips pouted extravagantly.

"Are you feeling all right?"

She—it—nodded. Christ, this was difficult. The sexy mannerisms, like the toss of the hair and the sudden expansion of the chest, kept throwing him off. Maybe he should leave this one to Lindi. But, of course, it was his job, not hers.

"You were in the, uh, carrier."

The eyes went blank. Carrier was not a word in its vocabulary.

"The cage?"

A shake of the head, still not understanding.

"Downstairs, in the basement."

A sudden smile, explosive, like a baby girl being of-fered some candy. "Basement!"

"Yes, basement."

"Yes. With blanket." The word blanket was said with a velvety tone that implied that it—*she*—really liked the blanket.

"Likes her blankie," sniffed Lindi.

"Look, this isn't easy."

Lindi chuckled. "Getting a hard-on, boss?"

"Shut up."

Lindi was still grinning as she turned back to the screen in front of her.

Venner studied Plesur. She was fiddling with a scrap of paper, a docket slip itemizing her entry into the HudVal PD evidentiary system.

"Do you know when you went downstairs?"

A shake of the head.

"Was it this morning?"

A smile. "Yes, 's'morning."

"Okay. Did Plesur go downstairs some other time?"

A serious look. She was straining to understand him.

"Did you go there before today?"

Again the sudden shaft of sunlight across the sultry face, the pout replaced with a dazzling smile.

"Yes. She come. Man say, 'Get blanket,' time go downstairs. She come."

Venner shivered suddenly, as if chilled by good luck. Here was a bolt from the blue, a sudden break.

He exchanged a look with Lindi, who flashed him a thumbs-up.

"Who is 'she'?" he asked very carefully.

The eyes brightened until they sparkled. It was a remarkable effect. The emotions in a Pammy were simple and powerful. When Plesur smiled, you wanted to smile, too. When her eyes shone, you just wanted to hold her, kiss her, be with her.

"Is this 'she'?" Lindi displayed her handheld in front of Rook, showing the sec cam frames.

"She is nice. Like Plesur," the mod continued.

"Like you?"

"Kinda." A little smile this time, self-satisfied, almost smug. Rook realized that Plesur thought that she was actually "nicer" than "she," whoever she was. Of course, in this instance, "nice" meant inordinately voluptuous and extremely beautiful.

Plesur's eyes shone with the simple, pure joy of being what she was, incredibly "nice." Rook understood. They had to be capable of laughter and sorrow. They had to have the prime human emotions, because it made them what they were. They had to be able to enjoy pleasure in order to be able to give it.

"Girlfriend?" Lindi asked Rook.

"Could be."

Plesur was studying him. She had a question of her own. "Where is man?"

Man?

"Oh." Rook rubbed his chin. How to tell her the truth. Especially since Plesur herself was an illegal form of life. Expensive, but doomed. As soon as the case was disposed of, she would be put to sleep with a lethal injection.

That is, she should be put to sleep. But it was one of those funny little facts of life that this very rarely happened. Someone or other higher up the food chain would wangle a way to take her home.

"I'm sorry, Plesur, but man is dead."

"What is dead?"

Great. Did they really have no comprehension of death?

"He has gone away."

"Back soon?"

"No."

Plesur's pretty face crumpled into a frown. "Who Plesur help now?"

A heavy throbbing sound pulsed through the walls, rapidly growing louder until it shook the building. Gunmetal letters reading FBI descended from the sky as a Mark 1 gunship landed outside.

"Your party guests have arrived," said Lindi.

"Shit! Take Plesur to the tac room. Get her in some other clothes."

"New clothes?" Plesur asked, with renewed sparkle in those fabulous baby blues.

"Nothing too exciting, don't get your hopes up," Lindi replied, leading the pleasure model by the hand down the corridor.

"And keep it quiet. Don't let the scum see her."

The scum were the worst of the legacy cops, political

appointees who regarded policework as just a way to make money, usually by bribes.

Venner glanced out the window at the Mark 1. It was all angular planes, matte black stealthmat with green lights strobing so fast it hurt to look at them.

The gunship dropped a ramp with a faint clang. A seven-foot-tall Thunder Claw combat robot sprang out like some huge insect made of metal and expensive polymers.

The thing's head spun slowly while its multifaceted eyes mapped its surroundings. A chestful of weaponry was ready to demolish the neighborhood at the slightest provocation.

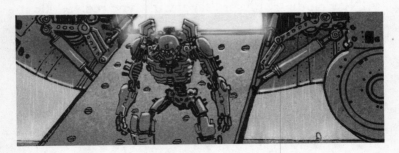

It took the visitors a while to find Venner, but they did.

The lead agent had a tag reading "Skelsa" on the front of his slick gray suit. Rook thought it was real nice they still had names rather than numbers. The rest of Skelsa was not so reassuring. Six foot six, he had a bucketful of implants including the weird inhuman eyes that were so common in the FBI these days. The agents were busy scanning the room, as if it, too, were a crime scene.

Meanwhile the damned combat robot filled the doorway like a fat man in a midget's suit. For a long, horrible moment, it focused on Rook and a green laser beam ran up and down his face. The thing had added him to its target d-base.

From where it sat on his desk, his Nokia was doing its own scanning. In his left ear the cool, Scandinavian voice reported a list of interesting discoveries.

"Senior Special Agent Skelsa has forty-one percent polymerization of skeleton, including leg bones, arm bones, and skull. First Agent Porter has twenty-six percent polymerization of skeleton. There's an ITL 44606 ID chip located behind the right ear, plus an Update RFID in his upper right arm plus three unidentified items. He is armed with a tac five-point-five with fifteen round mags, and tri-po sonic grenades."

"SIO Venner?" said SSA Skelsa, in that oddly warm, artificial voice. It was like some friendly old-time radio

DJ, always cheerful even while he was threatening to eat your children in front of you.

Rook avoided having his hand crushed by only offering his fingers.

"Please, sit down." He had two chairs and a bench, just enough room for these oversized humanoids.

"You are the lead investigator on the Sangacha case."

"Correct."

"What have you got?"

There was that famous cyborg bluntness.

"Before I answer that question, I have to ask you if you've cleared this interview with Area Chief Artoli?"

"That is irrelevant."

Venner smiled. "For you, perhaps, but not for me."

Artoli wasn't picking up. What a surprise. He left a message informing her that he had visitors from the FBI and would she please get in touch.

Then he had to tell them something. The state government up in Albany might want him to be uncooperative, but they weren't sitting in this office with a couple of semihuman things on the other side of the desk and a military robot lensing him from the doorway.

"Well, Senior Special Agent Skelsa, the truth is we have hardly anything. We have the victim. We know that he fired a shotgun three times and wounded, possibly killed, one of his attackers. We don't know how many attackers there were, and we have no leads as yet to their identities."

Rook made no mention of the pleasure model. He'd already decided to keep that piece of evidence to himself, at least until he knew more.

"DNA evidence?"

"Soon. But whether we'll get any matches or not I can't tell you."

Skelsa leaned forward. The act seemed threatening, even if it wasn't meant to be. "Put this on full priority, SIO. General Sangacha was an important man. There are enemies of the state at work."

Venner felt his eyebrows bob upward involuntarily. "Enemies of the state" was not a heartwarming phrase, nor something to lightly toss into conversation.

"No shit. Well, I'm sure you know more about that than I do." It was becoming very clear that he needed to get rid of this case as soon as possible.

Something about the tone of his response had not satisfied the SSA.

"I will expect your complete cooperation."

"Of course," Rook lied, doing his best to imitate the inhuman calm of the SSA.

"Let me know the minute you have the DNA work. Place this number on your inside list." A red light flashed on the Nokia's upper screen indicating forced data input.

Ingrid's voice protested in his left ear. "Violation of security code! Firewall activated." If a handheld could sound pissed off, the Nokia Supa did a good job of it.

Senior Special Agent Skelsa lumbered to his polymerized feet. Again Rook was careful to avoid getting his hand crunched.

"Keep in touch, Venner." The agent went out, scouting the corridor.

No sooner were they out of sight, clumping along the brown linoleum to the stairs, than Rook had Area Chief Artoli in his right ear.

"Venner!"

Wondering if there was a bug in his office that Ingrid hadn't picked up, he took a slow, deep breath.

"You're not a very good hostess, Chief."

She ignored that little thrust. "What did you tell them?"

"What I know. It was a short conversation."

"You were told not to cooperate."

"Check it out." He sent Ingrid's visual scan of SSA Skelsa. "Nice abs."

"Rook!"

"Yes, sir."

"What did you tell them?" Artoli pressed.

"That we didn't have anything much to go on."

"And?"

Rook let out a breath. "They told me to cooperate or else, and to tell them as soon as the DNA work is done."

"Which you will not do."

"Okay."

"That is an order."

"Okay, uh, sir."

"I'm sorry that I couldn't speak with them myself," Chief Artoli continued. "There's a lot going on right now."

"Oh, of course." Venner knew the game. She gave the orders, he got scanned.

With a thunder of engines, the Mark 1 lifted off, green lights strobing along the walls and windows as the huge metallic monster rose into the dark sky.

The rain continued to pour without the slightest hint of a break. Rook wondered if there would be mudslides along Route 28. He made a note to get the Nokia to check for him.

"One question, Chief. When they come back, how exactly do I tell them that I'm not cooperating?"

"You'll think of something."

CHAPTER 4

Rook found the pleasure model sitting in the tac room munching on a tofu-roast sandwich. Even a pair of gray sweatpants and matching hoodie couldn't hide her charms.

"Remember when we used to work with humans?" Rook asked.

"Those were the days." Lindi activated the wallscreen with a click of her handheld. "I ran through all the security footage."

"Okay."

"Lookee what we got here."

The footage displayed an image of a beautiful blonde leaving the service section in a green Nurida.

"She left just after the dazzle."

Lindi hit some keys to bring up another view, and a few seconds later they were staring at a blurry shot of the same blonde back in her car.

"Can you zoom in on the glasses?"

Another keystroke and the mirrored shades filled the screen.

"Distortion box." Rook pointed to a black square attached to the right side of the shades.

From the totally illegal distortion device, to the way the woman was keeping her face turned down and away from cameras, she was doing her damnedest to avoid the surveillance. But given just a little bit of info, the station AI could grind out some details. Lindi added some magic of her own and enhanced the image just enough so the mystery woman's firm chin and slightly hollow cheeks were clearly visible.

"I'm getting thirtyish, but could be older," Lindi surmised.

"Any ID on the car?"

"Not yet."

"Plesur?"

Plesur looked at them, and then at the screen.

"She?" Venner tapped the screen.

Plesur's pretty face lit up with another big smile. "Yes, she. She is nice."

"She comes over a lot?"

"Yes."

"How long have you lived with man?"

"Don't know."

"Thank you, Plesur."

The Pammy stared back at him, another gap in comprehension exposed, as in why did he need to thank her? All that cleavage made him uncomfortable. He needed clear thinking and Plesur was designed to prevent that sort of thing.

"Bad news, I'm afraid," whispered the Nokia into his left ear.

"What you got?"

"Car registration is fake. The plate number is delisted. Belonged to a Tommy Demarco, who is listed in Missing Persons. Disappeared five years ago."

"VIN?"

"The VIN does not match this car."

Rook turned to Lindi. "You getting this?"

"Yeah."

He went back to the Nokia. "Check that pic, see if you can find anything we missed so far."

He rubbed his chin, looked at Lindi, tried not to look at Plesur's cleavage.

"So this is 'she.' Her ride has fake plates and no reg VIN. What's that about?"

"She's in the business," Lindi guessed.

"You mean Sangacha wasn't satisfied with his half-million-dollar play toy, he had a regular pro come visit him, too?"

"Seems that way, unless we're missing something here."

"Let's see what else we can find."

"Right on, boss." Lindi went to work with a keyboard and the screen. Rook let the Nokia do the grunt stuff while he made phone calls here and there, looking for the telling details.

Over the next couple of hours a few useful things emerged. A textural analysis of the car's paint job revealed that it had been repainted from an earlier color, possibly white or tan, to the current green.

The vehicle was a Toyota Nurida, popular, but pricey due to the high-energy hybrid power plant.

The DNA work had come back without anything useful. The blood was from two individuals, Sangacha and an unknown who brought up no matches in the Fed d-base.

Rook tapped his ear piece. "Ingrid, anything on the blonde?"

"No matches in any database."

"If she's a pro, she's been a careful one. High-class call girl type, no crim connections, never busted."

"With a carefully disguised ride."

Rook stood up, stretched, yawned. Looked out the window. The rain had finally stopped. Huge puddles, jammed gutters, gushing streams remained. Darkness had settled in, leaving only pools of streetlights down Broadway where pushers waited to sell Dubl-oxy, Stresseptin, and Narcosoma, the favorite modern flavors of up and down.

Rook hardly paid attention anymore. It wasn't his job. It'd been offered, but he'd said no. That was for the legacies. So what if he never got rich, at least he'd keep his soul.

He looked at the old clock on the wall and decided to fold for the day.

"Okay, I'm done. Can't think anymore. Go home."

Lindi didn't need any encouragement. She started closing down screens and cutting out their link to the federal police net. Big AIs spoke to little AIs and everyone shook hands on encrypted super-protocols.

Rook went down to the washroom to splash some water on his face and get ready for the twenty-minute drive out to his little house in the hills. He was about done when Hesh Winnover and Fatso Soporides came in, giggling like schoolboys.

"Hey, Venner, you had any of the Pammy yet?" said Winnover. Rook glanced sideways and recoiled from Winnover's crazed leer.

"It's evidence," said Rook as grimly as he could. "On my case."

"Yeah, well, you don't mind if me and the boys give that baby a workout tonight. Hell, I've never seen one that clean." Fasto practically drooled. "Looks brand fuck- ing new."

Rook imagined Fatso having his way with Plesur. It wasn't a pretty picture.

"Pure sex machine. We are going to fuck that shit up." Winnover sounded positively gleeful as he rubbed his crotch.

"Sounds like quite a night, boys." Rook dried his hands and went back to his office.

"Rook, where are we?" Chief Artoli demanded in his ear.

"No matches on the woman. But her Nurida's been re- painted, so we're looking at matches in white, tan, gray, whatever."

"And how many of those are sold every year?" she asked dismissively.

"Millions."

"Uh-huh."

"Look, we still got the pleasure model," Rook offered.

"You think it knows something?"

"I need to find out and I can't leave it here overnight."

"Why not? It's safe in a cell."

"No, it's not. It's going to be raped."

Artoli almost laughed. "How can it be raped?"

"How do you think?" Rook responded angrily, then took a breath. "I can't risk getting her damaged."

"SIO, it's not human and it can't testify."

"But I can." He felt his temper rising again. "And I will, if this ever comes to trial. There'll be a full medical report on her. If she's badly damaged it will all come out."

Chief Artoli had gone silent. "Christ," she muttered. "Men are fucking animals."

"Chief, it's key evidence for my case."

"So take it home with you."

Damn. Yanking the Pammy out from under the noses of the legacies would stir up a shitload of trouble. But if he didn't do something, Plesur was going to see a whole new side of "man" kind.

"So what do you need?" Artoli asked.

"Call Kuehl at the front desk. Tell him to sign her out on my name and keep quiet about it."

A long silence ensued as the chief weighed things carefully. "I know nothing about this."

"About what?" Rook hung up.

That left the task of actually getting Plesur out of the cell, out of the block, out the door, and into his car without being detected.

It was time to call in a favor. Rook had an interesting network of friends, most of whom had rap sheets longer than his arm. He picked up the Nokia.

"Chaga."

"Shit a brick, it's the dick," said a cheerful, deep voice.

"Missed you, too. I need a favor."

"Of course you do."

"You'll like this one."

Ten minutes later, an automatic weapon let loose out on Broadway. The police station responded like they'd just sat on a nest of fire ants.

"Someone is out of his everfuckin' mind," roared Fatso Soporides. "You don't·go shooting off some Nine on our turf!"

More ka-thunks came booming from a few blocks away, amplified by a narrow alleyway.

"Jesus kee-*riste*!" Winnover jammed his tech hat on as he went galumphing by, shoving shells into a shotgun.

Rook went the other way.

Kuehl met him in the cells. "I got your prisoner ready for transfer."

He led Venner past a few drunks and fools in the holding tank, and a couple of teenage idiots who'd tried buying Dubl-oxy from Officer Wilhelm at the old mall.

Alone in number seven, Plesur lay in her blanket, fast asleep.

Rook woke her and helped her to her feet.

"Got to go, Plesur."

"Go?"

"Yeah, we have to hurry."

They went up the stairs, then ducked into a closet as

more cops went thundering down the main hallway, still buckling on riot gear.

Rook waited until the sound of boots faded.

"Come on." He pulled Plesur behind him and hurried her up the rest of the stairs to the ground floor and out to the carpark.

She was still bewildered when Rook put her into the front seat of his ancient Ford hybrid 4X4. He struggled to get the old gasoline engine started. He loved the old muscle cars, but this one needed some steroids.

The cops had started filtering back to the station. Chaga's little diversion had led to nothing more exciting than sweeping up some spent shell casings. The boys were disappointed and looking for action.

"C'mon, dammit." He tried the engine again. It coughed, sputtered, but would not start.

Cops were crossing the parking lot.

"Keep your head down." He pushed Plesur down on the seat, with her gold blond hair out of view.

Winnover had noticed the car, pointing to it and laughing. A standing joke with the legacies, of course. Honest cops being dumb enough not to take ready money and buy themselves decent rides.

"Fuck." Rook got out of the car and moved to intercept Winnover and his friends.

"What's all the noise?"

"Fuckin' zads, they're all morons," chuckled Winnover.

"When you gonna get a car that works, Venner?" Al Moranis, a legacy in Traffic, asked.

Winnover could scarcely contain his contempt.

"This baby's a classic."

Rook grinned.

Winnover's interest had flagged. He turned toward the station door. "Come on, boys. A night of 'Plesur' awaits us."

"Fuckin' ay," said Moranis.

Rook turned back to his car. That had been close. He couldn't afford trouble with the legacies. They had too many powerful friends.

Plesur looked up from the seat, eyes open wide. It wouldn't be long before Winnover and company found out that the Pammy was gone. They would suspect Venner, but couldn't be certain. By tomorrow Rook and the captain would have worked out something to keep Plesur safe.

He tried the engine again; it spluttered and finally caught. He breathed a sigh of relief, let it rumble for a few seconds, and then told the car to head for home. With a whirr the old Ford took off.

Plesur looked at him, blue eyes strained with anxiety. "Where go?"

"My house. You'll be safe there."

Rook decided to override the car's computer and took the controls himself.

"Unnecessary action!" flashed in green on the panel.

"Yeah, right," Rook muttered as he swung onto Chandler Drive and headed for the hills around Woodstock.

"Dark, there," muttered Plesur.

"Yes, not many houses where I live."

She was looking at him, but he was concentrating on the Route 28 exit.

"So dark," she said.

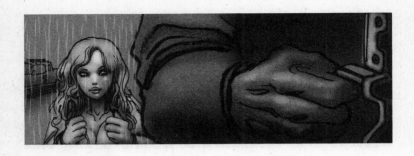

CHAPTER 5

Veriner's single-story ranch house sat on a two-acre plot way up on the edge of Catskill Park. There were neighbors, but they were distant.

Sensors recognized the car's approach and turned the lights on in welcome.

"Come on inside, Plesur." He helped her out of the car. Her anxiety had been replaced with intense curiosity.

"House?"

"Yes, this is my house."

Once inside he left her to explore while he tossed a couple of rapid-ready meals into the activator. Then he

changed into jeans and a sweatshirt and dug around for some clothes that might fit a Pammy.

She had found the bathroom.

"Shower?"

"Yeah, sure, go ahead." He handed her sweatpants, some clean socks, and a green cotton shirt. "Try these."

She gave him a look that was both mischievously coy and purely grateful. It was enough to melt a heart of stone and give a nonagenarian puritan an erection.

She closed the door and he got himself a beer and went outside on the back deck. The sound of rushing water filled the air. All the mountain streams were in flood from the rain. From the deck he had a view down to Ten Eyck and the huge new developments in the valley. Their lights were muted, all eco-friendly. This was the Incorporated Woodstock Territory, but he remembered when all that land had still been forest. The view had been better then.

A jumble of images fell through his thoughts like flakes in a snow globe. The Virgin Mary covered in blood. The

body of the general, covered in whip marks. The horrible leer on Hesh Winnover's face. And that damned robot standing in the doorway, lensing him for its d-base.

He took another swig on the beer, and let the case revolve slowly in his mind. This was where he often had his best insights. But did he really want to solve the messy murder of a general who served during the darkest days of the Emergency? He found enough trouble on his own, and cops who knew too much had a way of disappearing.

Wasn't like he had anything solid anyway. His only leads were a missing blonde and a pleasure mod with the IQ of a blueberry. The blonde could be a girlfriend, a pro. Someone who betrayed the general and let the killers in. Whoever she was, she didn't want to be found, and whatever Plesur knew about her, it wasn't going to include a home address and life history.

Loose ends, lots of them, and they might tie together in places he didn't want to go. Not even an SIO from the HudVal PD Homicide could tug those lines with impunity. At the very least it could get you sidelined into a desk job. At the worst, you'd be dead.

He chugged beer and tried to blank those thoughts from his mind.

He had other things to think about. Like Plesur's presence in his home. It had been a long time since he'd had a woman here. When Karen left, she had called him a lone wolf, and maybe she was right. The job didn't help. It always brought up the same questions with women, like that old favorite, "Have you ever killed someone?"

What could he say? Of course he had. He'd busted into hundreds of homes in the uninsured world, where people went for their guns before they said hello.

In those situations you didn't have much time to think, and sometimes people got killed. But women always looked at you differently when you told them that.

The beer was gone. He was about to turn around when he felt an arm slip around his waist and a warm body rub up against him.

"Man is sad?" whispered that husky little voice.

Christ, how did she know?

"Uh, well," he began, then lost that train of thought. Her head was resting on his shoulder, her hip nudging his thigh. It would only take a feather touch to send him out of control.

"Plesur is here. She help man."

Such an earnest statement, it made him laugh, and that saved him, pulling him back from the precipice.

"Thank you, Plesur . . . for helping."

Those incredible lips took on a slight pout. "When help?"

As in, "We haven't had sex yet." Oh fuck, talk about the fires of temptation.

"You have helped. Already."

The pout had turned to a frown. Then it was transformed into giggles and a strange little conspiratorial smile.

She push-punched him in the ribs. "You funny man!" The pushing turned to tickling and he ducked away, laughing. She came after him, face contorted in the pure glee of childhood.

And right there, as if outlined by a flash of lightning, he saw her revealed as exactly that, a child. Standing there in oversized sweatpants and T-shirt, she looked like a child lost in a world three sizes too big.

She exhausted herself trying to tickle him into submission until he finally maneuvered them both into the kitchen.

"How about dinner?" he said and popped open the activator to reveal a pair of Ezi-eatz, all hot and steaming.

Lindi always warned him against eating this stuff. "You have no idea what goes into that muck."

Plesur happily tore into her lasagna. For her it was good enough that it was hot and cheese-flavored. He ate his "beefanoff" and opened another beer.

After about a dozen mouthfuls, Plesur slowed down. "What happen?"

"What do you mean?"

"In when-when, mornin', we go?"

When-when, she'd used that construction before, and he'd understood it to refer to the concept of time, as in *tomorrow*.

"Yeah, we go to other place. Better for Plesur."

"Back to pleece station?"

He wondered if she'd picked that up herself, or if

General Sangacha had a thing for sexy policewomen. The more she understood the better, if he was going to get anything out of her.

"Back to police station for a little bit, then to another place."

"Oh." She seemed crestfallen.

"What's wrong?"

"No like pleece place."

And for a moment Rook saw in her wounded eyes what must have happened. Plesur sitting in that cell. Then the leering gaze of Winnover and Fatso Soporides when they came to check her out, their eyes feasting on the sexy meat they planned to chew on all night long. The terror she must have felt.

"I'm sorry about that, Plesur. I'll make sure it doesn't happen again."

The big blue eyes studied him. Did she understand him? Did it matter?

"Okay." She stared at him, waiting. "Help man now?"

"Hey, let's see what's on TV." Rook wasn't much of a virt fan, but he couldn't sit there while she stared at him like that.

"The Midwestern Combine Lottery is up to N\$2.5 billion!" the evening newscaster announced. "Forty million Chinese citizens have bought tickets."

The newslady chuckled. "The Chinese love gambling, don't they, Don?"

Don, the old, wise, silverback newshead, chuckled. "Good news for seafood lovers, cod is back on the market after twenty-three years of extinction. Folks say the genetically replicated fish tastes like chicken."

Rook hit the mute button and headed to the kitchen, rummaging in the freezer for ice cream. "You want dessert?"

When he returned to the living room the sound was back. Plesur had changed channels to one of the more lurid free-virt shows.

A sexy young woman was undressing while an overly muscled man helped her out of her clothing. The dialogue was breathy and short, all "Oh, Marly," and "I want you so bad, Jim."

Rook rarely used the virt interfaces. The helmet, gloves, and sheath stayed in the box. Virt sex creeped him out. It wasn't masturbation, because someone else was working inside your head, but it wasn't real sex either.

Not his thing, but plenty of men and women were addicted to it.

Plesur, however, was clearly an expert at virt.

On the screen, Jimmy slowly helped Marly out of her panties.

Plesur sat on the couch, rubbing herself with the end of the remote. The hair stood up on Rook's neck even while his dick hardened.

It would be so easy to surrender to his balls and just fuck the living daylights out of her. Christ, he wanted to, he wanted to really bad. And it was what she did—it was what she was made for, for fuck's sake!

Made for. Genetically engineered in some cold room.

He went to the bathroom and threw cold water on his face. "Oooh, oooh, oooh," came wafting out of the living room. This was fucking unbelievable. Trapped in the bathroom by the rampant sexuality of a pleasure model. He started laughing so hard he had to sit on the john.

"Man okay?" Plesur was right outside, a look of deep concern on her face.

He almost cracked up again, but the open worry in her eyes stopped him.

"It's okay, Plesur, I was just laughing about, uh, things."

The worry vanished and the huge smile turned on again. She took a quick step and hugged him.

"Plesur so glad man okay."

He stared into those blue eyes, so wide and inviting. The depth of her innocence was like a lance through his jaded heart.

The virt sex in the living room was being drowned out by ads for pain relievers and feminine products. Rook shouted, "Off," and was rewarded with quiet.

He took her by the hand and led her to the bedroom, showed her the bed.

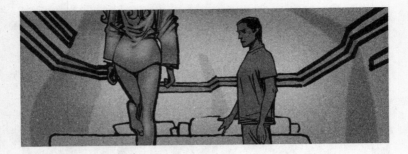

"Plesur help man now?"

"Plesur help man by going to sleep."

For a long moment she stared up at him. Had she not heard him? Or maybe she didn't believe him?

"Plesur bad?" Again the look of childish anxiety. As if she'd done something terrible.

"No, Plesur is good. Very good. But she'll help by sleeping here."

"Where man sleep?"

"Not man. Rook. My name is Rook."

"Rook."

"I'll sleep on the couch."

She smiled, seeming to accept that she would "help" later. "Rook nice man."

"Yeah."

He headed back to the living room where he checked his calls, interrupting the Nokia in the midst of a spirited debate on Strindbergnet on matters relating to *Inferno*, August's tortured novel.

As Ingrid emerged from the 'net, the screen was blazing with fiery red script.

"My souls (characters) are conglomerations of past and present stages of civilization, bits from books and newspapers, scraps of humanity, rags and tatters of fine clothing, patched together as is the human soul. And I have added a little evolutionary history by making the weaker steal and repeat the words of the stronger, and by making the characters borrow ideas or suggestions from one another."

"The active life of the artificial intelligence," said Rook quietly.

"We have to do something with all this time," Ingrid responded.

"You're probably gonna replace us in another hundred years anyway."

For a moment the Nokia seemed to vibrate in his hand. Ingrid was laughing. The first time he'd sensed that it'd been freaky, but now she seemed more human than a lot of people he knew.

"Talk to me about pleasure mods."

"What would you like to know? History, manufacturers, designers, fight clubs—"

"Fight clubs?"

"Owners pit their mods in combat. Rings have been recently broken up in New York, Shanghai, Delhi, and London, but clubs continue to flourish."

"History."

"Pleasure mods are an outgrowth of the Internet porn business that mushroomed in the early two thousands. Hiroto Jobs gene-engineered the first live pleasure mod, called Cherry, in 2020—you have a call message."

"Who?"

"Freddie."

"Who is that?"

"Unknown."

"Let's hear it."

There was the faintest click and then a message came through.

"SIO Venner, this is Frederick Beckman. I need to talk to you urgently concerning the General Sangacha case. This is a priority and you should employ full encryption when you return this call. My number is 44 77 88-900 766622."

Rook felt a little shaft of cold run down his spine: 88-900 was a priority code for the absolute top political elite.

"Who is Frederick Beckman?"

"Search underway."

Rook wandered into the kitchen, threw the leftovers from dinner into the waster, and wiped down the counters. He checked the fridge. Enough in there for a good breakfast for him and Plesur before he took her back to the station.

"Search complete. Report: Frederick Beckman, age twenty-eight, height six feet, weight two hundred and four pounds, hair brown, eyes brown. Son of Senator

Olivia Beckman of Oklahoma and her husband Neil Beckman. Born August sixth, 2040, Tulsa, Oklahoma. Educated at Ronder School and USC, left without a degree. Known as Freddie, young Beckman is a favorite great-grandnephew of Louisa Marion and a frequent visitor to Sable Ranch."

"What?" Rook grabbed the Nokia and read off the last line again. "Shit. You're sure about this?"

"Information obtained from public databases, confirmed by Internet search."

"Louisa Marion?"

"Correct."

That family's power went back to the beginning of the century. Rook didn't know the history; in truth, it wasn't taught in school or referred to on TV. National amnesia had kind of wiped the slate clean. He remembered his Granddad John, raging about something called "New Democracy." They were as "bad as the commies," according to him.

Of course, Rook wasn't too sure who the commies had been, either. And nobody in his generation was taught anything about the world beyond the borders. "America First and America Alone," that was the slogan drummed into them from first grade.

But you had to be a moron and completely free of content to not know the name Louisa Marion. There had been several presidents with the Marion name, or closely related; Rook couldn't exactly remember them, he hardly ever bothered to vote. You weren't encouraged to do that kind of thing anymore. But Louisa Marion, beautiful, shapely, with her trademark shoulder-length white hair, had been at the center of American political life for more than fifty years.

Rook took a deep breath and sat down. Where was this case taking him?

General Sangacha had played a role in the Emergency. His murder had brought down a visit from the feds. Now this phone call from "Freddie," a well-regarded nephew of Louisa Marion.

He'd already smelled danger; now he had red lights flashing and sirens wailing. What the fuck should he do? Call Lisa Artoli? Sit tight? Or call this Freddie with the high-end 88-900 number?

Sitting tight was probably not an option. Major powers

could not be ignored by such as Rook Venner. Calling Lisa Artoli made sense, except that she would do nothing if it was a risk to her.

Which left him with a single realistic option.

"Let's call him. Full encryption."

A few moments passed as red and green lights flickered on the upper face of the Nokia Supa.

"The line is busy. Sub-lines are also busy."

"Any way to leave a message?"

"Yes."

"Just say, 'SIO Venner is returning your call.'"

"Yes, sir. Good night."

Ingrid returned to the land of Strindberg discussions, while Rook settled in for a night on the sofa, thoughts whirling. It was unnerving to be stepping around the edge of a black hole with military and political connections in its depths. But after a while that fear slipped out of focus. Instead he was left with images from the day and the ones that stuck were the leers on Winnover's and Soporides' faces.

Human beings, feet in the mud, heads full of chips. Maybe it wouldn't be so bad when Ingrid and her pals took over. But would she still respect him in the morning?

CHAPTER

Angie Bricken, aka Mistress Julia, stared out the window into the night. Across the valley, maybe seven miles away, scattered lights broke up the darkness.

The house felt cold after the rain, and clammy. She had a call out to Doctor Jimmy, the only call she'd made since leaving Sangacha's place. If anyone could help her vanish, it would be him. Besides, he had given her the false plates. Sangacha's murder had been an organized hit, which meant there would be a thorough investigation. The cops were bound to run that license plate, find

it was bogus, and try to locate its source. She had to let Jim know those plates could be traced.

Her thoughts drifted back almost twenty-five years, to the day that changed her life. Mark's last message still echoed in her mind. "You have to leave town, right now. Don't come back. I love you. Good-bye."

She'd been so desperately in love. They were going to be married. She'd been twenty-five, with her whole life ahead of her. The bad days, the height of the Emergency, were over by then. If you were insured, you were supposed to be safe. People didn't disappear anymore. But Mark had done things that made him wake up screaming, or left him crying when he thought she couldn't hear him.

Young and foolish, she'd driven back to the apartment. She'd almost gotten out of the car, but at the last moment she'd noticed the two men standing in the alleyway. They were waiting for her, and in that instant she'd finally gotten it. Mark was dead and she was on their list, too. She'd

gone to the end of the block, turned right, and kept on driving.

So long ago. A lost world preserved only in her memories.

Eventually she'd made it to L.A., where Angie Bricken had morphed into Mistress Julia, professional dominatrix. It was a cash business and infinitely preferable to straight prostitution. There were no pimps, nor any actual sex. It was mostly a matter of attitude and mind games, and she was good at both, besides being blond and pretty.

She'd tried to find out what had happened to Mark. She'd managed to reach a friend, who'd served with him in D.C. and who was no longer in the military. There'd been a massive purge of former Special Forces people in the spring of '44—just when she had received Mark's last message. The friend advised Angie to stay hidden. "They're never gonna let up on you. They find you, you're dead."

But to kill her they had to find her, and so far they hadn't.

Up here on the ridge, she was known as Julia Rider. Her nineteenth-century farmhouse, abandoned during the military proscription, had been rehabbed by a New York artist, a grateful client of hers.

Doctor Jimmy's compound lay half a mile north on a road cut through dense forest.

The Doc was a fugitive from organized crime in London. He'd never explained, exactly, but a few things had slipped out over the years, usually when he'd had a drink or two. Angie felt a connection, as both of them were on the run.

Jimmy knew everybody, and he could get you anything, as long as you asked nicely and were prepared to pay the going rate. He could fix whatever was wrong with you, which was why he was the Doctor.

She prayed the people who hunted her weren't beyond Jim's scope. What choice did she have? The familiar terror settled like a shroud, ready to suffocate her. She had to run. Get out now and not look back.

The house computer gave a sudden beep of alarm.

Angie jumped, startled.

She glanced at the security monitor and saw a short, slender figure walking toward her house, wearing what looked like a jacket made of straw. That would be one of Jim's boys.

Mistress Julia opened the door before the boy could knock.

The youth stepped back. She saw a thin-faced boy of maybe fifteen wearing a hooded camo sweatshirt decorated with enough twigs and small branches that in outline he looked like a bush. "Got a message for Julia, she here?"

"I'm Julia. Who're you?"

"I'm Dip."

"Are you now."

"Jim says you're to come with me."

"Is he at home?"

"On patrol."

Damn. Her expensive running shoes would get trashed

in the mud. The house directed her to a pair of Wellington boots and a black waterproof hoody.

Outside she found the kid waiting down the driveway. She switched the house back to auto-lock, then set off in his wake.

They went upslope, north of Jim's house, skirting the high rock ledge and working through thickets of bamboo that had run riot all over the Hudson Valley. Twenty minutes later they were in a big grove of oaks. She saw a yellow gleam of light, seemingly coming from the ground itself, which turned out to be a shelter fitted into the roots of several big trees. In the hollow space, two more camouflaged teenagers sat with a bevy of high-tech equipment. Glowing screens seemed to float around their heads on the ends of wires.

"She's clean," said the nearest boy.

She caught the outline of a rifle.

A voice crackled out of the ether. "Kilo-foxtrot-delta, clear to approach."

A blanket slid aside and they entered a narrow path twisting between the dark trees. Everything smelled of earth and mold. Tiny red lights gleamed in the branches.

Along the way she spotted other kids, some who couldn't be over twelve, hiding.

Dip stopped beside a huge tree. "Here."

She looked around. "Where?"

She followed Dip's gaze. A dark mass about twenty feet up perched in the middle of the branches.

"Climb up on those." Dip shone a tiny red light on the tree's bark. She saw metal spikes projecting every foot or so in two rows.

"Jesus."

Julia climbed, one foot over the other without looking down.

Then she heard Jim's familiar Cockney accent just above her head.

"Jools, c'mon up here. Fings are really gettin' weird tonight."

She climbed through a trapdoor and found herself standing on a flat wooden base about ten feet long. She could see for miles in all directions, and the stars! Millions of stars were strewn across the night skies.

"What's up, Doc?"

"'Ello, darlin.'"

Jim sat on a fold-up chair next to a tent. He had a pair of massive binoculars in his hands and a tiny yellow light dangling on a wire a foot off his left shoulder. His big, slab-sided face cracked into a welcoming smile, acres of white teeth gleaming in the dark.

"Nice place," she greeted.

"Glad you like it. Top quality deer stand. Got it in Maine."

There was someone else up there with them. Another of the kids, she felt sure. The soft crackle of radio transmissions filled the night air.

"What's going on?" she asked quietly.

"Good question, that, Jools. Lotta activity tonight.

Had a couple of military drones roll over the ridge a while back. Then a chopper went north, came back south. There's all sorts of stuff on mili-net. Robots, you name it."

"This another one of your conspiracy theories?"

"Not this time, honey. There's a hunt and destroy team set up on Lalapa Mountain. We clocked 'em an hour back." Jim nodded in the direction of the mountains in the distance. "This is it, Jools, the big day when it all comes down."

"What are you talking about?"

"The fuckin' milit'ry dictatorship. You fink that's all over an' done wiv?"

"You tell me."

"Well, it ain't."

She shivered, despite the warm southwest wind. Jim had sources of information beyond her own understanding. How he had them, or even why, she couldn't fathom, but he seemed to know things that were inherently dangerous to know.

"Look, Jim, I need help."

His eyes glinted in the shadows.

"I have to hide and stay hidden."

"Got some trouble, then?"

"You could say that." Briefly, she told him what had happened at Sangacha's place.

"Fuck. Hid under the sink, didja?"

"I'm still alive. But they must have recorded those plates you gave me."

"Don't worry about it, love. The ponce what owned it is dead, see?" Jim scanned the horizon with the binoculars. "Where's the car now?"

"Here, in my garage."

Jim nodded to one of his lieutenants. "We'll take care of it."

Julia tried to relax a little.

"Sangacha . . . yeah. High-level military in some black ops unit buried so deep, you'd need a laser to find it. Had some mean fuckin' enemies. What are you gonna do?"

"I'm so sick of running."

The kid inside the tent at the end of the platform stuck his head out. "Captain, we got a trace on screen. Something's coming. Big un, too!"

Jim was up in a flash and into the tent, his weight shifting the platform. Julia did not like the feel of this. The height was starting to make her dizzy. Then she heard a low, distinctive throbbing coming from the east.

Over the ridgeline, a mile or so to the south, she saw a cross of red lights rise up and approach fast.

Jim emerged from the little shelter.

"Gunship!" he barked down into the woods below. "You got anyfing still turned on, get it off!"

The throbbing built, growing stronger. The cross of red lights came swiftly across the trees, low, ominous. Cold fear snaked up her spine as a massive shadow blacked out the stars. For a fraction of a second, Julia caught a glimpse of something bulky and jagged, hunched and ugly, a twenty-first-century predatory monster, and then it was gone, just red lights once more, heading roughly north by northwest.

Jim had his binoculars up, studying the thing. The heavy pulse was dopplering now, diminishing quickly.

"Big cunt, that's for sure. Shark class."

"What's it doing here?" Julia stammered.

"I got no bleedin' idea. Bit overkill for domestic missions."

A tiny voice seemed to materialize in the air between them.

"Heading 6439, NNW, Lalapa Mountain."

Jim pulled in the tiny wire-mounted earpiece that had floated away from him.

"Where's it going?" she asked.

"Over Woodstock way."

"I shouldn't have come here." Angie's fear surged to the surface, cracking Julia's control.

"Well, dun' matter where you go, does it. Not when the whip comes down."

"I'm innocent!"

"No offense, darlin'," Jim chuckled. "You ain't worth a shark class gunship."

But maybe her client was.

The cross of red lights was far away now, approaching the valley toward the foothills of the Catskill Mountains, a dozen miles north of their position.

"Stay on her steady, mates," murmured Jim, either to himself or to hidden listeners on his network.

Then the flash came. Huge and bright, then small and very intense, down in a bowl of the mountains.

"Fuck me!" Jim put down the binoculars.

"What the hell was that?" she heard herself ask.

The thud and boom followed, small, hard, and sharp, flattening out, soon lost in the distance.

Jim's smile gleamed like bones in the yellow light. "Missile strike. There's still some snake in that ol' bottle, darlin'."

CHAPTER 7

Rook Venner never remembered his dreams. But this dream was oddly powerful. He was being hunted, and the hunter was relentless.

He struggled to move through a deep, warm place, a cave, but his feet stuck in mud.

A flash of cold steel moved between the shadows.

He could feel the hunters though he couldn't see them, heartless and cruel—and not human. Something wrapped around his ankles, pulling him deeper.

He couldn't move. He was trapped.

His heart seized with panic, terror, but there was no escape.

He woke up, sharp and sudden. It took a minute to recognize his living room, remember he was on the couch, but he wasn't alone. Snuggled tightly against him, molded to his back and thighs, Plesur snored softly. He could feel those heavy, perfect breasts pressing against his back.

A glance at the wall screen brought up the time, almost two. He'd been asleep for about four hours. He wondered how long Plesur had left him alone before migrating out here to the couch. She obviously preferred company.

Ingrid spoke in his left ear.

"You have a call. Frederick Beckman."

Rook disentangled himself from Plesur and stood up. "Put him on."

"SIO Venner?" said a younger man's voice with something of a Texas accent.

"Yes."

"I'm sorry to disturb you so early, but you have two minutes to get out of your house."

"What?"

"Leave now. Please take the pleasure model with you."

"How the fuck do you know this?"

"If you want to live, you have to move right now."

Frederick Beckman sounded completely nuts. But if he wasn't. . . .

Rook spun around; Plesur was still asleep. He pulled his pants on, jammed his feet into his shoes, slung his shoulder harness over his arm. Then he grabbed Plesur and lifted her up with one quick motion.

She woke up with a shriek.

"It's okay, Plesur, have to go now." He tried to keep his voice level as he spun around and headed for the back.

"Go?" Her arms wrapped around his neck.

He told the house to open the back door, went out across the deck, and put her down in the yard.

"Come on, we have to hide."

She was frightened now. But then so was he. He took her hand and they ran into the dark mass of trees edging his property.

Rook pulled Plesur behind a massive pine and turned back to check the house.

The world vanished into a blinding flare of light. The blast threw Rook and Plesur to the ground, debris raining around them. Rook pulled himself on top of Plesur to protect her, wincing as something hard smacked him between the shoulder blades and skittered away.

Rook squinted through plumes of foul-smelling smoke. His house was gone. Fragments of deck stood up like weird petals on the side of a huge, smoking crater. Close by was the top half of the washing machine, a white gleam in the smoky darkness. Shit, he'd just bought that. He helped a trembling Plesur to her feet.

"Glad I didn't redecorate."

A flash of green light dropped from the skies as metal claws crunched on the ledge of the smoking crater. He'd

seen that exact shade of green light before, in the doorway of his office, coming from the combat robot. Flames
flickered off its gleaming body, turning the lights of its
eyes to glowing embers.

And then it stood up. The mechanical beast was twice
as big as the one in the office. Artillery built into its arms
clicked and whirred, seeking targets.

Holy shit. He had heard of mechanical animals but
he'd never seen a combat robot like this! What the fuck
made Rook so important?

"Plesur, we have to go."

Holding Plesur's hand he pushed on into the woods,

trying to brush aside low branches. For a mod just out of the box, this was one hell of a first trip outside.

Behind the house the ground took a steep plunge to the stream where rainwater roared down the mountain in a tide of brown water and debris. Impossible to wade across the torrent, so Rook followed the stream south where it would flow under the main road in about half a mile. He paused at the edge of a deep gully.

Plesur's hand tightened in his. "Green light," she whispered.

Moving through the trees, maybe a hundred yards away, sharp beams pierced the darkness as the hunter robot leaped in giant strides, heading straight for them.

"Sorry about this," he whispered harshly.

He grabbed Plesur around the waist and jumped into the darkness. They landed hard on the rocky ground, Plesur's muffled groan of pain echoed by his own.

Above, twin green laser beams scanned where they had stood.

Rook wondered grimly if the thing was targeting his ID chip. The monster moved downstream past their position—it didn't seem to sense his chips, or Plesur's.

A low thrumming sound interrupted his thoughts. It got much louder and a black shape covered in bright red and white lights rumbled above the trees.

The thing was huge, obviously a military gunship.

He got to his feet and pulled Plesur up beside him.

"C'mon, Plesur, we have to move."

He caught a momentary glimpse of her face, composed in an expression of utmost seriousness, trying her hardest to understand what was happening, and then she followed him.

There was a road somewhere back here that went up into the mountains. If they could find it, maybe they could hitch a ride. Or at least walk down into Woodstock.

And then what?

God knew who was after him. Actually it might be better if God didn't know.

He thought about calling Lisa Artoli. But she couldn't do anything, and the tin soldiers might be tapping her calls. Better they thought he was dead. He would stay off the radar, get down low, and hide. And he knew just the place, where he could call in some long-owed favors.

They crested a hill. The gunship was working its way down the stream, searchlights blazing in the darkness. The sight filled him with dread. They were checking for survivors.

A quarter mile farther on and they came to the road to Woodstock.

Just as he was about to step out of cover, he heard a weird little whine, as if a servomotor was misfiring. Green laser light panned across the trees above their heads.

As Rook watched, horrified, the green light caught a few strands of Plesur's golden hair. He grabbed her and pulled her down into the dirt.

Too late. The bark above them exploded off the tree. The whole world seemed to shatter as he rolled over with Plesur in his arms, the tree toppling inches from them.

Rook yanked Plesur up and scrambled through the vegetation, trying to keep his feet and stay in motion.

A startled raccoon broke from the trees and scuttled toward the road. A moment later it simply disintegrated, blown to fragments by the robot's machine guns.

Rook flattened himself against a tree, with Plesur pulled tight against his side. He could hear her breathing coming in little gasps. She was trembling, terrified. But she didn't cry out. Maybe she didn't realize that people screamed and shouted when they were scared.

The combat robot was coming fast, bounding along in fifteen-foot strides. It landed with a deafening crunch, checking out the kill. Its laser eyes probed the steaming remains on the gravel.

In about five seconds, the robot's sensors would detect them, and then they'd be scattered on the road alongside the raccoon.

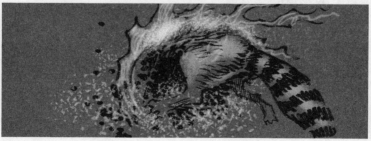

And then he heard the trickle of water almost beneath his feet. He bent down and saw the dark hollow of a culvert that ran under the road. There was just about room to hide in there. He shoved Plesur into the hole, then followed, crawling inside.

The rank smell of algae, cold and slimy, filled his senses. Rook prayed there weren't any snakes, but nothing stirred in the humid darkness. He moved up beside Plesur, and cradled her in his arms. "Ssh," he whispered in her ear.

Heavy footfalls thudded above them, and the distinct rasp of metal on pavement. The metal monster stood directly overhead.

Rook waited, the sound of their breathing impossibly loud in the enclosed space. The thing might miss him on its chipscan; there was at least fifteen feet of solid earth between him and it. Perhaps a minute went by, and then came that machine whine, another thud and then more of them, then silence.

He decided to take a look. Leaving Plesur in the darkness, with a whisper to stay quiet, he slid down the slime-covered concrete and crawled outside.

Wind rustled through the trees, the crickets kept up their steady hum. Cautiously he got to his feet and climbed back to the road. By the light of the moon he saw sharply cut tracks in the pavement where the robot had stood. It had gone. They were alone.

CHAPTER 8

"SIO Venner, you're alive?" exclaimed that voice with the Texas accent.

After thrashing through the muddy forest with Plesur for the last three hours, staying out of sight, wondering what the hell was going on, they were a quarter mile away from their destination. Just when he could almost feel the warm shower and taste the hot coffee, Beckman had called. And Rook wanted some goddamned answers.

"What the fuck!"

"I take that as a yes."

"My house is gone!"

"We are not in control of every aspect of this situation."

"No shit."

"Nothing is what it seems on the surface, you understand?"

"It *seems* like the feds tried to kill me with a fucking gunship!"

"Not officially. However, SIO Venner, your life remains in danger. You must listen to us."

"Who the fuck is us?"

"The Ranch."

Sable Ranch. Christ, this was way out of his league.

"SIO Venner, one thing."

"What."

"The pleasure model, is it all right?"

"She's fine. What's it to you?"

"Listen, SIO, don't make any phone calls for a while. We don't know who we can trust right now."

"Why should I trust you?"

"Because I have need of you—and your friend—alive. I will be in touch. And take good care of the pleasure model."

The call blipped out.

Jesus, what was he caught up in? The feds were trying to kill him and the most powerful organization in the country was trying to help him. What did they find so damn interesting about Rook Venner, SIO? He didn't know anything the rest of the cops on the case didn't know.

Rook shook his head, muddy water dripping off his hair, his shoes, his pants.

Plesur wrapped her arms around herself, pulling the wet green shirt taut across her breasts. "Cold."

"Yeah, I can see that."

Rook stared, then blinked. The only thing that separated him from the others was the evidence he had smuggled out of the station. It was Plesur they were after. Fuck! Winnover and Fatso probably ratted him out when they discovered their all-night party missing.

Rook turned around and pointed to the corners of a swooping Chinese-style roof. "We're almost there. Think you can make it?"

Plesur nodded.

Hide at the whorehouse—there was a certain logic to that.

Ten minutes later they stood at the front door. Rook reached for the Chinese doorbell, but before he even touched it the whole door glowed within the faux wood and turned to a slab of gold, while soft sec-lites came on. A quiet chime sounded inside the house.

"Rook?" The door opened a crack; behind it were two jet black, almond-shaped eyes, a tiny upturned nose, and red lips parted in surprise.

"How's tricks, Soozie?"

"Still out of your range." The door opened, revealing a slim woman wrapped in a golden silk robe, teetering on gold open-toed sandals. Her dark hair was held up with golden skewers.

"You and your friend better come in."

The interior of Soozie Kong's Wayside Inn was warm, and lit by subtle glows coming from panels hidden in walls and ceilings. Spicy incense hung in the air.

Soozie was sizing them up with calculating eyes. "What's going on, Rook?"

"That is a very good question. Could really use a shower, Sooze."

Soozie clapped her hands. A middle-aged Chinese woman appeared from the shadows, wearing a gray tunic. "My guests need a shower, and clean clothes."

The servant led them upstairs to separate suites where they could clean up.

Rook let the hot water steam away the slime from his hair and back, while he thought about what he was going to tell Ms. Kong. Since his involvement in a case five years earlier, when a well-connected client managed to kill one of her girls, Rook had made the occasional visit to the Wayside Inn. Not, however, for the usual reasons men went there. In the original case, Rook had withstood some not-so-subtle pressure to drop the charges against the client and pursue charges against Sooze instead. That didn't happen and it was the beginning of an interesting friendship.

When he stepped out of the shower, she was there, sitting on the bed wearing nothing but a teddy in the same color gold as the robe.

"Feeling better?" she asked with a sly grin.

"Much. But I need clothes."

"Oh, I don't know, you look good without them, SIO Venner."

Sooze stretched like a cat. Whether her looks were the result of surgery or purely natural, Ms. Kong was a beauty, and she knew it.

He grinned back. "That's a relief."

She stood and came to him. "I didn't know you were into Pammys."

"It's not like that. She's involved in a case."

"Tell me another one," Soozie laughed.

"Someone doesn't want this case solved."

"And you're risking your life for that?"

"Not quite . . ."

Sooze had one hand on his hip; the other slipped between his legs. "Just talking about that little critter got you excited, unless . . ."

"What?"

"You're just glad to see me?"

"Always."

Plesur, the gunship, his house, all fell away as she slid

to her knees. Maybe she was only doing this to keep her cop protector. And yet there she was with his dick in her mouth and loving every moment of it.

He picked her up, carried her to the bed.

Setting himself between her legs, Rook started slow, came quickly, restarted with barely a moment's hesitation, and took his time on the second go-round. Soozie's hands held tight to his ass, as she kissed him and bit his neck in equal measure, arching her back, crying out. He let himself go and the flood poured out of his veins,

shaking everything within him and leaving him spent and, for the moment, oblivious.

He rolled over and found a pillow under his head, and Soozie curled up beside him with her head resting on his chest.

"It was your place they blew up, right?" she whispered.

"News travels fast."

"Lot of people saw the flash."

Rook eased himself up to his elbow, staring into her dark eyes. "Everyone scared?"

"You bet. Nothing like that for years."

"But you're not."

"I'm an adrenaline junky." She tapped the end of his nose with a long red fingernail. "You always bring the best trouble."

He moved her hands away and sat up. "I got a case that somebody powerful doesn't seem to want investigated."

"What kind of case?"

"Murder, what else?"

Sooze draped herself against Rook's back, her breasts soft and warm against his skin. "You're safe here, of course, but if I was you, I'd consider having your chips pulled before you leave."

The Wayside Inn possessed high-end and totally illegal jamming systems, so Sooze's clientele could visit without leaving any electronic traces. Which was why Rook had headed there in the first place.

"That's a felony. I'll be classified as rogue."

"Won't matter if you're classified dead," she breathed into his ear.

True. Rook rubbed his eyes. Christ, he was tired.

Sooze pressed a tiny gold stud in her right earlobe. "Cindy Wales," she said. A few moments passed as the call went out. Sooze stroked Rook's chest with one hand.

"Cin? Sorry, terrible timing. Sweetie, I need a favor. Yeah, now."

Sooze smiled, ran her left hand in between his legs.

"I'm a cop."

"Not anymore. So pay up."

Rook found the stimulation more than he could resist. His hands cupped her firm, round breasts. She raised a leg and straddled him. She was wet, ready, and he slid in with a single smooth flexion of her hips.

"Cindy's coming over right now. She'll take them out for you."

"Thanks."

Sooze began to ride and Rook forgot everything for the next few minutes, until they were both finished and lying there sated.

"You know," she said with a mischievous pout, "I should've brought your little Pammy in for a threesome."

"She's evidence. Don't touch."

"Evidence?"

"Sooze, curiosity, you know?"

"What, killed the cat?" Sooze swung her feet to the floor, slipped into a silk robe and strode to the window. The first rays of the rising sun peeked through the drapes.

Rook turned on his side and shut his eyes. "You don't want to know any more, believe me."

"That dangerous?"

"Ask my house."

"Pity, she seems very fresh. I would wager not two weeks out of the crate."

"And you've seen a lot."

"It's my stock-in-trade, sweetie. Most are just worn out, ready to die. And when they get down to the last couple of years . . ."

He didn't say anything.

"You wouldn't believe what men are capable of," Soozie whispered bitterly.

"Actually, I would," he said before letting the world slip away into the darkness of sleep.

CHAPTER 9

Rook sat at an antique lacquer desk, gazing out the window at the placid waters of a small lake. The afternoon sun shone languorously over smooth stones in the Zen garden. It was nice here. Too bad he wouldn't be staying. "I need to call my assistant."

"Sure, use my system." Soozie walked in from the bathroom, brushing her hair in long strokes. An emerald green dress rippled over the smooth curves of her body.

"It is safe?"

Sooze chuckled. "With my customers? Some are phoning while they fuck. They never stop."

"Check systems," he told the Nokia.

"I detect a satellite link to Deng 9, Chinese telcom sat."

"Get me MacEar."

She picked up before the first ring was over. "Boss, you're alive?"

"I believe so."

"They said you were killed. What the hell happened?"

"Someone blew my house up. Gunship dropped a combat robot to make sure."

"Holy shit! This was official?"

"Don't think so, but then I don't know what is."

"Who else knows you're alive?"

"Nobody."

"The chief?"

"Best not to tell her. Not yet, anyway. In fact, let's just keep this between you and me for now."

"What about the pleasure mod?"

"She's okay, she's with me. Anything more on the car?"

"I got forty-seven thousand direct matches on the paint job."

Rook sighed. That wouldn't lead to anything, guaranteed.

"I was going back to the crime scene," Lindi continued. "Talk to the staff, see if anyone had an ID on our blonde."

"Okay, but be careful. Whoever's on the other end doesn't mind killing cops."

"Boss, where are you?"

"Safe location, that's all I can say right now."

"How do I get in touch?"

"I'll set up a bump account."

"How about flowers?" she suggested.

"Good idea. Embed the audio in the left side of the pics."

Rook told the Nokia to find a good online sharing site and set up an account.

"What name would you like to use?" the smart phone asked.

"Randomize something."

"It's 7rt65rst19tom67 then."

"Got it," said Lindi.

"Later."

"Doctor Cindy's here, sweet cheeks."

Rook turned to find Soozie eyeing him like prime beef. He was wearing a white terrycloth robe provided by Sooze's servant. He wanted his own clothes back, but they were still in the drier.

The door to the bedroom opened to admit a plump lady in a business suit, carrying an expensive-looking metal case. She set it down on the side table.

"You're the one who needs chips pulled?"

Rook nodded. He had been a cop for twelve years, a good cop. But that was all about to change. Once the chips were removed, he would be classified rogue and a wanted man.

Doctor Cindy produced an instrument that looked like a cross between a hair dryer and a pistol. "If you'd just remove the robe."

"What?"

"Hold onto the family chips," Sooze laughed.

"Fine." Rook dropped the robe, grabbed a towel, and tied it around his waist. "Okay?"

"Very good, sweet cheeks." Doctor Cindy passed the device over his body, about half an inch above the skin. When it passed over a microchip it flashed green and mapped the location, whereupon the doctor used a small marking tool to put a blue circle on the spot.

In less than five minutes she had everything marked. He looked like a damn constellation.

"You'll feel a jolt with each extraction. You want a tranq?"

"No. Just do it." Rook had had chips extracted before, during a bout of chip-sick. He hated the narcotics. Pain kept him sharp.

The extractor made a soft hum, punctuated by a little thud as it yanked a chip.

Rook took his mind somewhere else.

"Quite a haul there." The doctor held up a little jar. "These are dead now, no one can trace them." Rook took it and glanced inside at the half dozen tiny silicon devices. The doctor ran a sterilizer over the little blood spots on his shoulders and back.

The door opened suddenly to reveal Plesur, wearing white pajamas and carrying Rook's cleaned and dried clothes.

"Plesur bring Rook his clothes," she announced with a big smile.

"Thank you, Plesur. How are you feeling?"

"Better. Needed to sleep. You?"

"Good." Rook turned to the doctor. "Would you mind running a check on her?"

"Of course." Cindy adjusted the chip location device. "Plesur, remove your top, please."

"Okay." Plesur undid two buttons and slid the pajama

top off. Her magnificent breasts swung free. Rook blinked, then looked away.

While Doctor Cindy checked Plesur for chips, Rook took his clothes into the bathroom and got dressed. When he emerged, the doctor was packing up her stuff.

"Anything on her?" Rook asked.

"Nope, not one. That's unusual. Owners usually stick at least an RFID in them."

"Yeah." If Plesur was carrying information, it wasn't stored on a standard chip. What was so special about the Pammy? What was worth sending a gunship and combat robot after her?

"Thanks, Cin." Soozie escorted her to the front door. "You're an angel."

The doctor chuckled. "This mod is very clean."

"Yeah, so you said."

"No, I mean, it hasn't been touched."

Rook stared at Cindy.

"She's a fucking virgin!" Sooze howled. "Oh, man."

Rook slumped into a chair as Cindy left. Sangacha hadn't even slept with the mod. If he never wanted her for sex, what the hell was he using her for?

Nothing in this case added up. A virgin pleasure mod being chased by a gunship, and for what? She couldn't even tie her own shoes.

Plesur had found a small bedside TV screen and was deep into a sex virt, giggling as Buddy went down on Bonny, only to find that Bonny wasn't really a girl. Well, she looked like a girl, except between her legs. Plesur found the look on Buddy's face perfectly hysterical as he came up for air.

"Silly man," she shouted at the portable virt screen. Then she saw Rook, got up, and ran to him. The pajamas were gone, replaced by a pink top and a pair of white jeans. Rounding this out were some comfortable-looking low heels.

"New clothes," he murmured.

"You like?" She struck a pose with her breasts pushed out and one hand on her hip.

"Very, uh, nice," he said.

"Yes," she crowed. "Plesur is nice!"

"No doubt about that," said Soozie with a chuckle.

"Thanks, Sooze, probably saved my life."

"You owe me one more." Soozie grinned like a cat that'd had the cream.

"What?"

"I made some calls. This guy, Sangacha, right?"

"How'd you know that?"

"Honey, when it comes to gossip who would know better than the owner of the best little whorehouse in Woodstock?"

Rook nodded. That was a good point.

"He was a big man, down in the city."

"And?"

"He liked to fuck guys."

"Anyone in particular?"

Soozie nodded. "I'll take you to Nancy's. There's someone there you need to talk to."

"What about her?" Rook glanced at Plesur.

"Oh, she'll fit right in, believe me."

CHAPTER 10

Manhattan rose out of the night like a vast creature made of lights. A backbone of the new supertowers stuck up in the center of Midtown, while older, smaller towers were crammed cheek by jowl from the Hudson to the East River.

Plesur, of course, had never seen anything like it, except on TV. She stared out the window with eyes wide, mouth slightly open as they raced down the Palisades.

Soozie's pricey little Beemer got them to the city inside half an hour, using the high-speed lane, right next to the roaring, rocketing freight traffic.

"You didn't have to take us in," he told Soozie.

"Hey, I haven't been down to Nancy's in too long. I have some things to talk over with her. I've been thinking about getting a male pleasure mod."

"A male one?"

"There's a new kind, called Alberto. Very cute. Perfect for the older gay market in Woodstock. Nancy has all the connections in that world."

"I bet."

Rook and Soozie were prepared for the programmed swoop down into the tunnel at more than a hundred miles an hour, but Plesur was not. The car slipped off the Palisades' power rail with no more than a soft clunk, diving into the Lincoln Tunnel entrance. One moment they were heading toward the candy-colored towers across the Hudson, the next they were in the white, claustrophobic world of the tunnel with a thousand other cars hurtling along like shotgun pellets in the barrel of the gun.

Plesur screamed, clutching at Rook's chest.

"It's just a tunnel, Plesur. It goes under the river."

She was staring at him, terrified, and then understanding filtered in. "Tunnel," she whispered.

The traffic around them slowed down at the same rate, smooth and easy as they rolled in lockstep up the East Side ramp and out into the blinding glare of nighttime Midtown.

Plesur stared out the window, completely absorbed in the passing scene. Shop fronts, pedestrians, the sheets of glass and steel soaring up into the darkness, the huge logos flashing on and off in the sky, it was all new to her, and utterly fascinating.

Big helium-filled ad floaters slithered by overhead, lights flashing, advertising scrolling across their bellies.

Soozie parked in an underground lot and led them around the corner and down a set of stone steps. A red door opened into a pulsing atmosphere filled with noise, alcohol, a faint odor of sweat, and a variety of fragrances. Pink and amber panels glowed in the low ceiling and the tables along the walls. They took a table toward the back, where Plesur watched the dancers on the raised dance floor as they flexed and spun, thrust and wobbled, looking like well-oiled automatons.

Soozie was well known here and well-wishers, male and female, came up to hug and kiss. While the dress code was about as relaxed as possible without actual nudity, none of what he was seeing and hearing shocked Rook, who had extensive experience in the uninsured world. What did drop his jaw was their waitress. Her face was an exact duplicate of Plesur. Every detail from her wide blue eyes to her pert little nose. She was a Pammy, but as different from Plesur as someone with identical genetic makeup could be. Her hair was short and black, her bosom had been flattened by surgery to something approaching a normal size, and her eyes had a hard cast to them that spoke of worldly awareness. When she spoke it wasn't with Plesur's soft little burr, either, but a flat New York accent complete with attitude.

"Hi, I'm Ivana. What can I getcha?"

"Marijuana," said Soozie briefly before turning back to a young black woman in a tight-fitting suit of golden spandex. "And not that medicinal shit, either."

Plesur stared at the waitress, astonished. For a long moment the pleasure models locked eyes.

"And you, sweetie?"

"She'd like something nonalcoholic."

The waitress snapped Rook a look of black fire from those baby blue eyes. "You make all her decisions, do ya, daddy?"

"No."

Plesur was still staring at the waitress. "You just like me."

The waitress sniffed. "Sweetie, I am you, and you are me." She wrote something on her pad. "Strawberry smoothie, okay?"

"Yeah, fine," said Rook, feeling embarrassed for some reason. "Look, I . . ."

"You don't have to give me any excuses." She was waiting for him to order something. "Beer?"

"Uh, something light."

"Light." She looked at him again, hard, before heading to the bar.

The idea of Plesur giving Rook that kind of

contemptuous look was outlandish. But this mod seemed like a normal working woman.

Soozie broke away from a group of young men by the bar to whisper to Rook. "Don't tell me you never heard of a mod upgrade."

"Not common in my line of work."

"Easy, daddy. This place has equal rights for mods. Don't go getting all twentieth century on me."

"I'm an old-fashioned kind of guy."

"You are a funny one, Detective Venner."

"Who she?" Plesur breathed, still recovering from the shock of seeing herself.

Soozie leaned close. "She's a waitress. Do you know what a waitress is?"

Plesur looked up, confused. "No."

Rook put his hand on hers protectively. "It's okay, don't worry about it."

Her lips parted in a slight smile.

He glanced at Ivana, filling their order, chatting with the bartender. And suddenly a realization hit him. What if Plesur were smart? He could drag her around and never get answers until a bullet gave him one. With an upgrade, maybe she'd know why everyone was after her. Maybe he'd have a shot at saving his own skin. And maybe there could be some kind of life for Plesur, too.

"I'll be right back." He walked to the bar, sliding past rows of partygoers.

Ivana was loading her tray as Rook approached.

"Can I have a word with you?"

"Don't you have enough on your plate?" she shot back.

Rook flashed his detective shield. The light flickered suspiciously in those deep blue eyes.

"You've got the wrong idea." He put the shield away. "I just have some questions."

"Check Mediawik. I have work to do." The waitress hoisted her tray full of drinks and turned away.

"Wait." Rook caught her elbow. Her look could have frozen hell.

"Sorry." He quickly stepped back, arms raised. "Please. She needs help."

They both glanced at Plesur. Ivana waited.

"*I* need help. The mod is involved in a case. Could be very dangerous for her."

Ivana set the tray on the bar. "Katie, can you take these to table ten?"

"Sure, honey." A short redhead smiled brightly and took Ivana's tray.

"Three minutes."

"What happened?" asked Rook.

She looked at him for a moment. "To me?"

"Yeah."

"You really don't know?"

"I wouldn't be asking."

She turned her head to one side and tapped a little ruby-colored bead of plastic set behind her right ear.

"You've never seen one of these before?"

"Earbunk."

"My intelligence is just as good as yours now. Probably better."

"No doubt."

Ivana smiled. "There are more of us than you think, Detective."

Rook stared into her deep eyes, full of intelligence and understanding.

"Look, I just want her to be, well, whatever she can be. Okay?"

Something in Ivana's eyes softened noticeably. "Talk to Nancy."

And suddenly she smiled. Plesur's smile, but loaded with irony, concern, even understanding. "Be careful what you wish for, daddy. She won't be the same. Certainly not your little Pammy anymore."

"She deserves better."

"Don't we all, brother."

CHAPTER 11

Jim's farmhouse was an electronic rat's nest crammed with old-tech computers, monitors, scopes, meters, and antique rock posters. Using the obsolete equipment meant Jim could fly under the radar, undetected by the modern sensors.

Reaching behind a mass of cabling, Jim pulled out a bottle of whiskey. He poured a small measure of amber liquid into snifters. The stuffed bear in the corner of the room seemed to grin a little wider as the whiskey swirled.

"Here's to a long life, darlin'." Jim tapped his glass

against hers. They made a solemn sounding "dong," like bells. "An' a 'appy one."

He took a sip and so did Julia. She hadn't touched liquor in twenty years, but the explosive cascade of malt and honey flavors took her right back.

"That's yer real Speyside Malt, darlin', forty years old."

"Amazing." Julia felt the alcohol rushing to her head and set the glass down, sinking back into the leather couch. It might be delicious, but it would undo days of careful anti-aging work. "What are we celebrating?"

"The day I've been waiting for is here!" Jim announced.

"Funny. Feels like the day I've been dreading for twenty-five years."

He took a slow sip. "It's all a matter of perspective."

"You got that right. I'm thinking Seattle."

"'Ang on, Jools. You can't run. Not this time."

She glared, blue eyes turned to fire.

"Nah, 'ear me out. Your general gets murdered and a

few hours later there's a shark in the skies. I dun' believe in coincidence."

"I didn't know he was a general. I'm not sure if they knew it was me in that apartment or if I'm just collateral damage."

"Just tidying up."

"They're gonna get me no matter what I do." She tried to smile, to summon back her confidence.

Jim grinned in a conspiratorial way. "You don't fuck with the girls with whips in their 'ands. You can take control of this situation."

"It's not so simple."

"Never is."

She stared across the table, handmade like everything else in Jim's crazy-quilt cabin.

"So, darlin', let's get down to business." Jim topped off his glass with the forty-year-old single malt. "Tell me what I'm missing."

Julia slid away as Angie let the memories come. She hadn't spoken of Mark to anyone since the early days in L.A. "A long time ago they . . ." She hesitated. "Some secret group killed my fiancé, and they would've killed me if they'd found me. But I got away. I've been hiding ever since."

Jim sighed, leaned back in the big wooden chair. "Why'd they kill 'im?"

She shrugged and took another sip of the whiskey. "He knew about stuff that went down back in the thirties."

They sat there a moment in silence.

"Jools, this Sangacha is—*was* one motherfucka. Lot a blood on 'is hands."

"You think there's a connection?"

"Crossed my mind." Jim suddenly leaned forward. "Who did yer man work for?"

"He never told me what he did. I know it was military," she said slowly, eyes wide in realization.

"What, like Pentagon special forces?"

"Something like that.

Jim held up his glass, catching light in the amber liquid. "Cleanup unit, as it were."

"And I'm a spot they missed."

"Well, look on the bright side." Jim glanced at a softly beeping monitor. "Maybe the entire organization what

134

killed your boy 'as retired by now. Or they're dead. Like Sangacha."

Angie blinked. Wheels spun in her mind. Was that even possible? This was such a tantalizing, wonderful idea. "I could stop hiding," she said in something approaching a whisper.

"Or maybe you're right." Jim's eyes narrowed. "Maybe you're on the list. One way to find out for sure."

"How?"

"You 'ave a client that could tell you things."

She raised an eyebrow. "I have a lot of clients."

"This one's special."

"You don't mean . . . ?" she asked, horrified. "I swore I'd never go back to that perverted son of a bitch."

Jim beamed.

CHAPTER 12

In Nancy's the drinks came and went. Rook was feeling a little light-headed. Soozie had disappeared somewhere. Plesur leaned against the bar between a pair of men who were acting up just for her. Plesur seemed to get these people. She understood things sexual, even if she didn't have the vocabulary.

"Silly man!" she giggled. The men entertaining her roared in laughter, delighted.

Plesur was just a piece of evidence; she had no rights. When the case was over she would vanish. Powerful men would want her. Men who were vastly more powerful than Rook Venner.

And why should this bother him? Why the fuck should he care? There were always new cases, new problems, new horrors to deal with.

Give it a few days and who'd remember little Plesur?

There was a tap on Rook's left shoulder. He turned and found a well put together lady in a black suit, fishnet hose, and perilously high heels studying him with sharp brown eyes. Her hair looked cheap blond, but he was sure it was expensive.

"I'm Nancy Pell, this is my place."

She had the ageless look so common these days, and he pegged her as being in her thirties.

"Rook Venner, SIO, Hudson Valley."

"Soozie told me. I have a few cops as customers." She glanced in the direction of the waitress. "Ivana said you wanted to know about mental enhancements for your pleasure model."

Rook nodded warily.

"I didn't know Manuel had one." Nancy's red lips twitched in amusement. "He was full of surprises."

"So I'm learning."

"Why do you want this?"

"She could help me find the killers."

Nancy studied him for a moment.

"Mods are worse off than slaves. You upgrade her, all the nasty things come flooding back. It's a shock. Some of them cry for days. Others don't cry at all, they get . . . angry."

"She's . . . never been kissed."

Something in Rook's tone of voice seemed to please Nancy.

"I know a lotta cops, SIO Venner. Some are okay, some are worthless, and some are just plain bad. You don't seem to fit into any of those categories."

"A regular knight."

Nancy shrugged. "All I ever see is people with their hands out."

Rook shrugged. "I have to keep her alive. Might be easier if she was upgraded."

She chewed her lip for a moment. Then made her decision. "My friend runs a small clinic over on the East Side. It's very discreet."

"How much?" Rook asked, unsure how he was going to pay for this.

"A lot." Nancy smiled and shook her head. "I'm sure we can figure something out."

Very true, thought Rook. He was sure she would find some use for him. He was sliding away from the world he knew. Closer to the kind of person he'd spent his career hunting down and locking away, and all over a pleasure mod. But it was the only way to stay alive long enough to discover the truth and maybe save his life.

Something beeped softly. Nancy tilted her head. "We can probably get this set up for tomorrow. Soozie is always welcome to stay at my place. You and the mod are, too, of course."

"Thanks." He watched her walk away, firm derriere moving her tight skirt like a fine clock. He glanced over to check on Plesur.

She was still being entertained by a shifting cast of men and women, laughing and flirting. They were drawn to her like moths to a flame. They couldn't help themselves.

Tomorrow she'd be a different person, a whole different animal.

But he wasn't going to change his mind. She deserved the upgrade, no matter what.

He saw Soozie working her way through the crowd with a young man behind her. She had a big grin on her face.

"Rook, this is Pipo Haman. Pipo, meet Rook Venner, the detective investigating your boyfriend's murder."

Haman's slinky, shiny green suit hugged his muscular young body. The handshake was soft, the inhumanly good-looking face sculpted by surgeons.

"Poor Manuel." The accent was New York born and bred. "What happened to him?"

"That's what I'm trying to find out."

"He was killed." Plucked eyebrows flattened into tight little lines. "That's all we heard."

"Shot, multiple times," Rook confirmed.

"I know he had enemies."

"For instance?"

"You know, from way back, when he was in the military." Pipo's eyes darted anxiously.

"He spoke about that?"

"Sometimes . . . he would cry. We'd be drinking, and he'd get all moody."

"Do you know why?"

Pipo hesitated. Rook watched him as he struggled to find the words.

"Being a believer, that made him very guilty, very worried about his soul, you understand?"

"You visited him in Peekskill?" Rook continued his questions.

"Yeah."

"Did you ever meet the pleasure model?"

"Oh, god, that thing? I've known tomatoes that are smarter."

Rook detected an undeniable undertone of jealousy. Interesting, if not necessarily informative. He switched tacks.

"So how did you and Sangacha meet?"

"Right here, I think. Or it might have been at the Dance Garage."

"Sangacha was cruising?"

Pipo's soft lips flared in contempt. "Of course. Manuel liked to fuck. But he *really* liked to fuck me."

"Okay."

Rook sensed that Pipo was a little disappointed at the policeman's easygoing acceptance of that last statement. Why the young man would think that a seasoned homicide detective would blink at the idea of men fucking each other was a bit of a mystery. Pipo clearly needed to get out more.

Pipo kept on talking. "One time he said something about the Pammy, that she could blow them all up. I thought he was joking."

"Who might them be?"

"No idea. And another time he woke up from a nightmare shouting about blood and babies. He scared me. He was so big and strong. But I held him and he kept saying over and over that he was going to bring them down."

"Where was this? Peekskill?"

"Oh, no, in the apartment."

"What apartment?"

"Our place. Under my name so no one could find him." Pipo smiled. "Our own secret hideaway."

"You still have it?"

The anxiety was back in Haman's voice. "Around the corner."

Rook felt a door open on the case. No one knew about this place. If he stashed any secrets, it would be there.

"Would you mind showing me?"

"What, like, now?"

"Right now. Might help me nail the people who killed him."

That registered with young Pipo. "Okay."

Leaving Plesur under Soozie's watchful eye, Rook followed Pipo through the kitchen and out the back.

On the street, the late-night crowd paraded by in full display. Pipo walked beside Rook with a jaunty step, exchanging greetings with several other young men.

Pipo stopped outside a little restaurant, Bistro Lascaux. Even at this hour customers crowded the tables. He pointed to the top floor of the building.

He put his eye next to the security plate and the door swung open. They climbed a flight of steps where another door opened into a spacious loft, a large party room with a bedroom and bathroom at the back. A leather wet bar took up one wall and velvet couches lined the others. Everything was expensive and indulgent, definitely Pipo's style.

The art on the wall was unfamiliar to Rook, who wasn't exactly up on modern art anyway. He noticed painted scenes of an arid landscape, each overlaid with sheets of clear plastic, shimmer-screen style. The piece suddenly shifted, and the desert was replaced by a group of houses with swimming pools. And then it shifted again. The pools filled with sand, swallowed by the desert. The houses were gone except for a pole here and a concrete slab there. Rook looked more closely. The new scene was on the overlay, a cyber-image. Underneath it he could still see the desert landscape.

"They change constantly," said Pipo. "The Euridiki's worth about two mil."

"No shit." Rook had found a locked door, just past the bedroom. "What's in here?"

"Private office. He didn't like anyone going in there."

"Can you open it?"

"Yeah. Hold on."

Pipo pulled open a drawer in the bedroom and rummaged under the neatly folded shirts.

"Here." He handed Rook the key.

The small room had been modeled into a cyber-station, with an old-fashioned household computer, a wraparound screen, and a keyboard. To the right side was a bookcase stuffed with real books, all on military history themes. Titles jumped out at Rook: *Stalingrad—Battle of Destiny*, *The Eagle and the Snake—Vietnam*.

In the desk there were files; one held the lease for the apartment. Another held some faded photographs. One showed a couple standing outside a modest single-story

adobe house. The man was brown-skinned, Mexican, perhaps with some Native American, too. The woman was pale, with brown hair twisted into a braid. Behind them a small truck sat in the driveway. On the back it read: "Papa grande y abuela Britney."

A humble background, then. Rook found another pic, more recent, sealed in plastic. A young man in military uniform, every inch a soldier, standing before a low green building with a flagpole outside. The Stars and Stripes fluttered from the pole, and another flag, blue and gold, flew beneath it.

"The general?"

"Yeah, such a stud."

Rook had to agree with that analysis. The young Sangacha had the same broad shoulders as the older version, but his handsome features were unmarked by the deep lines the future would bring. Confidence shone in his dark eyes, challenging the world. Rook bet the older Sangacha's eyes had looked a hell of a lot different.

The drawers below the computer were not locked either. Rook found a pistol, a Smith & Wesson .38 with four clips of ammunition. Underneath lay account printouts from a private bank—Morclay and Son, of White Plains. Rook flipped through them. That was interesting. How did a retired general get one hundred thousand dollars transferred into his bank account every month?

Two-million-dollar artwork on the walls. A mysterious income of more than a mil per year. That wasn't a military pension.

Which meant he was working for somebody—but who?

In another drawer Rook found a black box, and inside that an official badge. A fist holding a short sword and the words "Interservice Special Selection" embossed on its face.

"Any ideas?"

"No. Never seen that before." Pipo shrugged.

Then Rook saw a slim steel box, about the size of an old-time cigarette case. He pulled it out and held it up in the light. From behind him, a loud voice warned, "Get out or I'll blow your fucking head off!"

Rook whirled around, pointing his gun at—a fish mounted on the wall.

"Drop dead, motherfucker!" the fish screamed.

"What the fuck is that?" Rook exclaimed.

"That's Manuel," said Pipo, smiling.

"Quite the catch." Rook put the Nokia on the job. "Check this machine out, see if you can find anything that might be pertinent to the case."

The computer's lights blinked on as Ingrid got to work.

"Warning." Ingrid's Scandinavian voice immediately sounded. "Attempt to penetrate the security wall has triggered an alarm."

Rook stepped back. He swung the door shut and locked it, but took the key.

"Come on, we better get out of here."

Pipo, who wasn't privy to communications from the Nokia, was taken aback. "What's happening?"

"We've tripped an alarm. Don't suppose you know how to turn it off?"

"What alarm?"

"Thought so. Let's go."

Rook propelled Pipo through the door and down the stairs.

Outside they crossed the street and hid in an alleyway. The bistro was still humming with activity.

Pipo slunk against Rook's side, nervously eyeing the building. "What are we doing?"

"Shut up, stay still. And move over."

Minutes ticked by. A few customers strolled out of the bistro, a gaggle of young women sauntered by, but nobody noticed Rook and Pipo hidden in the shadows.

And then a black van hurtled down the street and screeched to a halt outside the restaurant. The doors opened and a heavily armored SWAT team poured out.

The door to the stairs popped open with a loud *crack* and a small cloud of smoke.

"What is that?" whispered Pipo.

"Shaped charge. They blew the door. Now shut the fuck up!"

Another bang came out of the building; the lights went on upstairs.

"Let's go," said Rook, fingering the silver case in his pocket. "I think we got what we came for."

CHAPTER 15

The mirrors in the completely redone Chelsea Hotel in lower Manhattan were the latest in smart-mirror technology, designed to detect your mood and show you what you wanted to see. They were hugely popular, but pricey.

"After this I'll run away," Angie told herself. "Go where no one will ever find me."

Angie switched the mirrors off. Who she needed to see was already there, staring back at her from the plain glass. Someone completely in control, unafraid, steeled to risking everything. The small part of her that still fought the transformation slipped away.

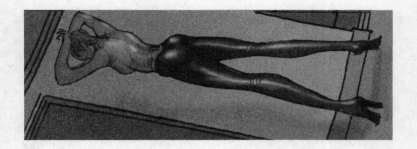

"Fuck you." The image in the mirror spoke menacingly. "I'm here now."

The black leather pants went well with her hair up. Eyebrows dark, lips bloodred, Julia was every inch the successful dominatrix.

There was a click in her ear. Her call was being returned, as expected.

"Hullo there, been quite a while," said a warm male voice with something of a Texas accent.

"I've been travelling," Julia lied smoothly. "Bet you'd love to see the present Auntie brought back for you."

"Damn, but you're right about that. All work and no play makes me a dull boy."

Mistress Julia chuckled. The role here was that of the strict, beautiful Auntie, who liked to make her nephew happy. And since he had needs that were a bit perverse, Auntie had to go to some lengths to indulge him.

"I have free time this evening," she said, reeling him in with her voice.

"I'll clear my schedule."

"Here at my hotel?"

There was a brief pause as he considered his options. "No, here. I have to be careful right now."

Careful? What did that mean?

"Shall we say seven?"

His voice was a hoarse whisper. "Bring a fresh girl. No marks."

It was good to hear that confidential tone in the client's voice, almost pleading for compassion. "I always deliver."

"That you do."

"See you at seven." She hung up.

Julia knew her client's desires could never be spoken of within his world. He liked to see a girl with a virgin ass getting her first whipping. There was something special in the screams, the sobs, and the sight of the red lines surfacing on pale white skin that did it for him. And afterward the whipped girl had to blow him a couple of times while he drank champagne.

But the client was unpredictable. Sometimes he needed to take it further. Sometimes he killed them.

Mistress Julia was a professional; she didn't allow personal feelings to interfere in the business. Angie, however, had never quite gotten past her disgust with this client. But when you were pandering to an ex-president of the United States, you held your nose and did your job.

The only difficult requirement was that he needed virgin ass. Smooth, white-skinned, unkissed by the whip. She pressed the call stud. "Get the Frog."

A few clicks later and a weary man's voice came on.

"Where the fuck you been hiding?"

"Miss me?"

"I miss your money."

"I need a girl. Has to be white, and perfect. Virgin ass."

The Frog whistled. "Expensive ass. Ten large."

"Make the call."

Mistress Julia studied herself in the mirror again. The leather worked, but the hair might be better down, and she'd need the long gloves. As for the whip, she'd brought three choices. The simple, single-tail, kangaroo hide "Striper" that she'd used for many years. It brought up

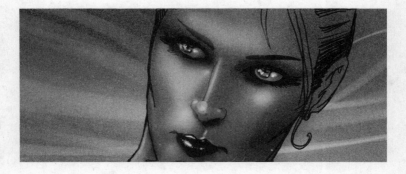

nice welts, but rarely cut the skin. There was a longer, heavier "Desperado" bullwhip, which was actually more show than substance. And then there was a bright scarlet coaching whip that produced the most amazingly loud cracks and snaps. For the sound effects alone that was the whip to use.

Probably, though, she'd use all three, in a session that would last a good long time. For the girl, who'd be hanging from the hook in the door frame, it would be an eternity, but her agonies were an essential part of the game. Because afterward, when the client was softened up, partly drunk on champagne, relaxed by some blow jobs, Julia would sit on the couch and cuddle him to her breasts. That's when the answers would flow like rain over the cold ground.

CHAPTER 14

Nancy had a lush loft just across the street from the New Chelsea Hotel. A high-end furniture store occupied the ground floor with ten lofts above. She had the tenth, at the top of the building.

Rook, Plesur, and Soozie were sharing the guest bed, which was big enough for six. Rook hadn't even bothered trying to convince Plesur that she should sleep on her own. She was snuggled up on his right side, while Soozie lay on the left.

"Long night" was Rook's last observation before his

head hit the Helthillo. The pillow contoured itself instantly to his head.

There were no dreams, only the deep oblivion of exhaustion. Somewhere, rising from the black, there appeared an oddness, a sense of something wrong fluttering on the edges of awareness.

Rook woke with a start and reached for the gun he'd stashed under the pillow. Beams of sunlight broke through the thick drapes on the window. Outside, cars rolled down the street, hitting a manhole by the corner with a regular clank. A horn sounded from the direction of Eighth Avenue. Inside, nothing seemed to be stirring.

But Rook's police instinct told him something wasn't right.

He slid down the bed. Plesur made a soft snort and rolled over; Soozie didn't move.

Rook crouched by the door. Nancy had cut the floor space into four areas. The bedrooms took up the back; a music studio was set up in the front. The main space was open, with a walled-off kitchen, pantry, and exercise room on the east side of the loft.

He pulled the door open a crack. Daylight filtered in from the high windows above the partition walls. He was looking down the corridor between bedroom suites toward the big open space.

He pulled the door open wide enough for him to slip outside. Nothing, except a draft of air along the floor. He moved across to the other side of the passage and hid in the doorway to the bathroom. What the hell was it? Why was he standing out here half naked with a sidearm in his hand? The soft click was the only sound as he slid the safety off.

He edged along the wall, eyes peeled, ears straining for the slightest sound. Nothing. Nothing at all, except another distant car horn out in the street. Nothing . . .

The punch came with a tiny grunt of effort and Rook's flinch saved his life. Instead of smashing his nose and driving the bones into his brain, the invisible fist slammed into his cheek just below his left eye.

Rook's head snapped back. His body caromed off the wall and bounced away as a foot meant to smash his Adam's apple crashed through the wall. Staggering, he brought the gun up and squeezed off two shots, the deafening cracks echoing off the high ceiling. He heard a grunt, a curse, and then out of nothing there appeared a

tall humanoid figure, clad head to toe in silvery white material, with a single rose of red, mid-torso. The eyes were silver like a giant fly.

It went down on one knee. Rook fired again and the man toppled on his side, blood spilling freely across the material of his plasmonic suit.

Rook had heard rumors of invisible assassination squads, run out of Washington, D.C. Plasmonic material bent light around the wearer.

Where there was one, there would be others.

Rook raised his gun, scanning the hall, but there were no targets.

Nancy ran into the living room holding a little silver handgun, her eyes wild. Plesur stood behind her, terrified.

"What's going on?" Soozie stood at the bedroom door, then saw the guy on the floor. And the blood. She screamed.

Rook tried to hush her and was kicked hard in the chest.

He fell as the air exploded from him. It felt like his heart had turned into a rock. He heard Nancy fire her pistol, but could barely move, struggling to get breath into his lungs. Something shattered on the wall. He rolled, took another boot, this time to the shoulder, and felt the gun kicked out of his hand.

He tried to get up and was kicked back down, hard.

And then he saw Plesur with a lamp in her hand. The lamp exploded. Someone cursed. Plesur was slammed against the wall, but Rook had his arms around an invisible leg and pulled hard. The assassin went down.

Another shot was fired and something crashed to the floor. Rook scrambled for his gun, rolled to his knee, and fired in a smooth single motion. Instantly another guy materialized as if out of thin air. Blue sparks rippled over the silver plasmonic suit. A round red hole in the center of the chest collapsed the guy like a balloon with a slow leak. He folded up, crouched, then fell over.

Rook didn't fire again, worried that he was getting low on ammo. There was a spare clip, but in his jacket. "Everyone all right?" he called out.

Soozie stuck her head out the bedroom door. "There's another one. Smacked into Nancy."

"Plesur?"

The Pammy was crumpled up by the bathroom door. Rook edged toward her, keeping the gun up, ready to fire.

"Nancy?"

Still no answer. Where was the third assassin? He could be anywhere. Rook tasted blood; his lower lip was split. His chest hurt; he hoped he didn't have broken ribs.

He bent down to check Plesur's pulse. Still strong. She shook her head as she regained consciousness.

"Plesur help Rook?"

"Yes. You did." He smiled.

She smiled back.

"We have to get out of here," he said. Soozie was in full agreement on that score.

Rook slid along the wall, eyes straining for the slightest hint of the third man. At the door to Nancy's room he pulled back, then swung inside, gun aimed at chest level, his finger squeezing down on the trigger.

Nancy lay on the floor. Her gun glittered beside her, caught by a shaft of light through the blinds.

She struggled into a sitting position, saw Rook, and waved a hand weakly.

"You shot someone?"

"Two of 'em." Rook stayed in the doorway, scanning the bedroom.

"I saw something run, like an outline of a man."

Rook turned carefully, aiming down the passage into the main room.

"You think they'll be back?" she asked.

"Certain of it."

Plesur had pulled on some clothes. Soozie tossed Rook his shirt and jacket and he slammed a fresh clip into the gun.

Suddenly the elevator doors banged open outside the loft.

"This way!"

Nancy ran across the living room and into the walled-off kitchen. She flung open a door into a dark passage.

"Where's it go?" Rook asked.

"Fire stairs."

The doors to the loft smashed open behind them.

"Run!" Rook pushed Plesur through the door. The window beside him exploded and he heard choked-off thuds coming from the living space. He wheeled and fired back. There was nothing to see but the couch and chairs. The kitchen cabinet beside his head splintered. He ducked, pushed through the door, and leaped up the narrow stairwell.

Nancy swung open the door to the roof. The Empire State Building loomed ten blocks away. To the south the grand old Hotel Chelsea reared above them. Directly in front of them there was a gap, and then beyond it an ocher-colored brick building.

Rook looked around for something, anything, to jam the doorway.

The roof was bare. He heard feet on the steps, leaned in, and fired around the corner. Someone screamed; bullets gouged holes in the wall beside the door. Rook jerked his head back.

Plesur stood at the edge of the building, her hair streaming out like a mat of gold.

Rook fired another round down the stairwell. More thuds answered as bullets smashed bricks.

Rook stepped to the edge, looked over. There was a gap of fifteen feet, but the other building was a story lower.

"It's our only chance," he said to Nancy.

"Christ, I don't know."

He grabbed Plesur by the shoulders, looked her in the eyes.

"Have to jump, okay?"

"Plesur jump."

"Look out!" screamed Soozie.

The door was opening. Rook fired into the gap. The door swung shut again.

Rook pulled Plesur back to the edge.

"Run as hard as you can and then jump. When you land, roll. Understand?"

She nodded.

"Go!"

Plesur took off, sprinted to the edge, and leaped, arms windmilling as she flew out across the empty space.

Rook slammed the door shut again. It wouldn't be long before the killers broke through.

Soozie ran over. "She made it!"

"Got to do this," he said to Nancy. Soozie nodded agreement. Both women had removed their shoes, but Nancy was keeping hers in her hands.

"Go!" Rook ordered.

Nancy ran as fast as she could, and launched herself into the air.

Rook willed her across the space, praying she made it.

Soozie signaled that she had.

"Now you," he said.

Soozie turned, ran to the edge, and leaped into the air, arms flailing. A rifle shot rang out, sharp and hard, and she doubled over like a diver off the high board, folding up, then plummeting to the ground ten stories below.

Rook looked to the east and saw the sniper team taking position on a balcony.

He pumped three rounds in their direction, knowing the odds were against a sidearm. But it was enough to make them duck.

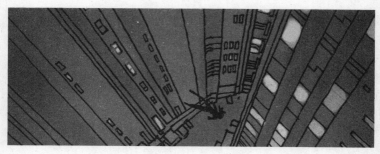

He ran and leaped. He was falling, expecting the bullet. Then he was below the edge of Nancy's building and out of the snipers' line of fire. He thumped down hard on the roof, tried to roll, and went over flat on his face with a jarring impact.

A moment later, Plesur was kneeling beside him.

"Rook okay?"

"Yeah, think so." He struggled to sit up.

"She gone." The pleasure model's cheeks shone with tears.

"Yeah. Lot of that going around."

CHAPTER 15

In the cab, hyperventilating, sweat pouring off his face, Rook struggled to get a grip as a cold band of fear ran through his guts.

He saw Soozie going down between the buildings, over and over, like a fucking video loop. Felt his heart sink with her.

All his fault. If he and Plesur hadn't shown up at her door, Soozie Kong would still be in Woodstock looking at her perfect little lake.

"Fuck," he whispered. "Fuck, fuck, fuck."

"My sentiments entirely," said Nancy, sitting on the

left side of the cab. She was still holding her high heels. "Who the fuck were they?"

"Had to be military," growled Rook. "Invisibility shit, nobody else has that."

Suddenly terrified that he might have lost it in their mad run to the corner, Rook went through his pockets to find the little metal file case. His Nokia was there, for which he breathed one sigh of relief, and then his fingers found the file case and he breathed another.

"I have to get this opened." He showed it to Nancy.

"Dangerous?"

"Explosive protected."

"What is it?"

He placed it back in his pocket. "Maybe an answer."

Plesur sat between them, recovering from the running, the terror, the jump off the building. Now she turned toward Rook and grabbed the front of his jacket. Her eyes seemed to bore into his.

"Plesur still get smart," she whispered.

Rook glanced at Nancy. She nodded affirmatively. "I'll see if they can take us early."

"Where you want to go?" said the cabdriver, who was already motoring uptown in medium traffic.

"Twentieth and Third, northeast corner," Nancy answered. Then she quietly made arrangements with the clinic.

Rook felt Plesur take his hand and hold on tight.

"Plesur get smart," he heard her say again as the cab turned a corner to head east and accelerated.

The clinic was hidden behind the Cityhealth Spa Center, where smartly dressed women came and went for their massages, facials, and more exotic treatments. The cab let them off near the alley on the side of the building. Nancy rang the back doorbell. A laser scanned her face; three seconds later the door opened.

There was a mirror-finish corridor ahead of them and Rook felt almost at home. The mirrors were part of a high-end security system that used super-intense LED lights and 140-decibel sound blasts.

"Mirror!" Plesur admired herself, looking from side to side. Reflections of her and Rook piled up on each other, receding to infinity.

They were scanned again by a green laser and then the door opened slowly on heavy gimbals.

Inside sat a waiting area in neutral gray and blue. A young woman in green scrubs emerged with a clipboard.

"Hi, I'm Gale."

"You the one I just spoke with?" Nancy asked, looking over the tech's shoulder.

"Yes. Joanne won't be in for another two hours but we're all set up for you." Then she turned to Plesur. "Do you know what's going to happen?"

Plesur licked her lips, shifting her eyes nervously to Rook. He smiled, tried to be reassuring.

"Get smart," she said in a small but determined voice.

"Exactly."

The girl passed Rook a handheld screen. It displayed a range of earbacks—little flesh-colored units designed to plug into the cranial interface. They contained microdrives that could hold anything from a set of languages to complete personalities, in the event that a pleasure model owner wanted a more entertaining, intellectual courtesan.

"We usually suggest the El-Plan forty. That's a forty-petabyte drive with the Onaguchi Interface and the Sony D-series port system. Guaranteed to provide IQ levels of one hundred twenty or above."

"That's a good one," Nancy told Rook.

"Okay." Rook imagined submitting his expense report on this case—if he ever got it solved.

"All right. If you'll come with me." Gale extended a hand to Plesur.

"What's the timeline on this?" asked Rook. "We're in a bit of a hurry."

"With the operation and recovery, about three hours. She'll be a whole new person." Gale smiled. "You have to sign these."

Rook hesitated. This woman seemed eager, maybe too eager. This facility ran under the radar. No one knew what was going on here—but he had no other choice.

"I'll take care of it." Nancy took the papers and rifled through them, signing quickly.

"I'll call when she's ready." Gale held up her hand-held.

The Nokia and Gale's handheld swapped numbers. With a last brave look over her shoulder, Plesur disappeared through a frosted glass door.

Once she was gone Rook pulled out the little metal file case and examined it carefully. There were a pair of

ports on the hinged end. He let Ingrid lens them with her little webcam.

A few seconds later Ingrid announced, "The device is a military safety file, designed for pilots and infiltration agents. It is armed with BeZixx4, a nano-polymeric blasting gel."

"Can you open it?"

"Possible. Seventy-five percent chance of success. But you would be incinerated."

"What about you?" Ingrid had been his only true friend. He'd hate to lose her.

"You can download my system from the main server—"

"But?"

"She will not be as pretty."

"What's it saying?" asked Nancy.

"It's private." Rook slipped the phone back in his pocket. "We have to go someplace where an explosion won't matter too much."

"How about New Jersey?"

"Too far," Rook answered. "Where's the nearest park?"

"Madison Square, just west of here, a couple blocks north."

Rook hesitated. "Think she'll be all right?"

"Nothing's been all right since you showed up."

"I'm sorry I dragged you into this."

"Well, here I am. Might as well go blow up a park while we wait."

Outside, they paused a moment as a cop car went screaming by, rack lit up, siren cleaving the air. It disappeared, heading west. Rook felt the tension slowly ratchet back up again. He wasn't on his own turf here. Getting targeted by the NYPD would be a really bad move right now.

Rook tried the number left by Freddie Beckman the night before, but got no answer, not even a machine. It was early in the morning; maybe Beckman was sleeping in.

They found an empty section of Madison Square

Park nestled in between a stand of leafy maples. Rook polished off the coffee and bagels they'd bought on the way.

"I guess this is as secluded as we're going to get." Nancy studied the throng of people strolling up and down Madison as she sipped her drink.

"If this baby explodes, it won't matter where we are." Rook hooked up the little steel file with the Nokia.

The phone gave a beep, and the green progress light flashed a couple of times. "The device is password protected, at least one thousand digits in length."

"Shit."

"It can be decrypted, but it will take time."

"How much?"

"Difficult to say. At least one hour."

"Get me MacEar."

Rook sat back, drank hot coffee, and mourned Soozie Kong.

He remembered the first time they'd slept together, and how good the sex had been. How Soozie's earthy, cynical humor had always made him laugh. He knew that at first she'd been playing him, turning the good cop into a useful shield for a whorehouse madam. But as they grew to know each other their relationship became something else, an occasional sexual thing eventually settling into friendship.

And now she was gone.

Beside him, Nancy had been talking to friends nonstop, filling them in on what had happened. She was meeting up with disbelief and resignation.

"Sergeant MacEar is on your online share-site," Ingrid announced.

"Boss! What up?" MacEar sounded relieved to hear that he was still alive.

"Here's what we have. Sangacha had another life. Apartment in the Village. Liked to pick up young guys."

"There wasn't a trace of that at Peekskill."

"There's more," Rook continued. "He wasn't as retired as everyone thought. Someone was paying him big dollars on a regular schedule."

"For what?"

"I don't know yet. What's happening at the station?"

"Very quiet, certain amount of paying respects. By the way, sorry you're dead, boss."

"Thanks. What'd you dig up?"

"Got some info on our general. He led an outfit called the ISS for a while. Must be the black part of black ops. All records stop five years ago. Don't even know what it stands for."

Rook fished in his pants pocket and came up with the badge he'd taken from the apartment. "Interservice Special Selection."

"You sure know a lot for a dead guy."

"I found a badge in his apartment. I'm thinking it was pretty special considering what's been going on the last few hours."

"*I'm* thinking they killed people," MacEar stated. "Like our vic."

"Look, MacEar, a team of killers came to get us this morning. Don't know how they knew where to find us, but they were wearing invisibility suits."

"Plasmonic suits?" Lindi sounded like she'd just met the Easter Bunny. "You really saw them?"

"No, that's the whole fucking point."

"Jesus, boss. What the fuck is going on?"

"There's a war going on and this case is part of it. Our job is to stay alive. Don't let anyone know you're working on this case. Check the office for bugs twice a day at least, and don't get followed home."

"What about the Pammy?"

"Dead like me. Keep your gun handy."

"Loud and clear, boss. Transferred the decrypt."

"Thanks." Rook killed the call.

"The password is a page of text," Ingrid informed him. "*King Lear* Act 5, Scene 3."

"I just can't believe this stuff," Nancy snapped to Rook. "Oranie's telling me to leave town, go to L.A. I hate L.A., I'm a New Yorker, goddamnit."

"Might not matter if you're dead."

"Of all the gin joints in the world, you had to wander into mine."

Rook raised an eyebrow. "And it looks like the only way out is to solve this case."

"How the hell are you going to do that?"

"Maybe in this little file case we'll find an answer."

A helicopter rumbled past overhead. Rook fought the urge to look up. "Don't show your face. Might be scanning for us."

The chopper moved south and Rook risked a glance up through the trees. He couldn't tell if it was civilian or

military, not that it would matter much since he didn't know who was actually trying to kill him.

The Nokia interrupted his thoughts. "There is a call. Frederick Beckman again."

"Connect."

"SIO Venner, you've been stirring up a shit storm."

"I noticed."

"We thought you were going to stay in Woodstock." Mr. Beckman sounded a little aggrieved.

"Yeah, well, I've been making progress. What's the Interservice Special Selection?"

"How'd you find that?" Beckman sounded alarmed.

Rook thought for a second. "Pentagon files. Sangacha ran the ISS for years."

"You are not cleared to know about that. That information should not be available."

"Well, it is. Now, you want to tell me what the fuck is going on?"

"That is impossible. You don't have clearance."

Don't have clearance. Soozie was dead, his house was gone, some military group was trying to kill him, whoever "they" were, and Mr. Fredrick "Sable Ranch" Beckman wasn't giving him any answers. If he really worked for Sable Ranch.

"Listen up, pal, I'll make my own clearance."

"You're going to get yourself killed."

"Already did. What's the Ranch doing about this? Can I get some help here?"

"I'll let you know. Policy is being decided right now. Good-bye."

"Shit!" Rook sat back. He and Plesur had nowhere to go and nobody to help them.

"What's the Ranch?" Nancy asked, looking worried.

"Sable Ranch, where Senator Marion lives."

"*The* Senator Marion?"

"There's more than one?"

"Excuse me," Ingrid interrupted. "Shall I proceed with opening the AM Dat-File case?"

"Do it."

"I would suggest that you retire to a safe distance. The explosive charge in the device is very powerful."

"Time to make some noise." Rook grabbed Nancy and stepped away from the bench, leaving the black Nokia hooked up to the metal file. Rook just prayed that nobody came along looking for a quiet place to eat a hot dog.

The Nokia spoke up. "SIO Venner, should I not survive this, may I say that it has been a worthwhile experience to serve as your smartphone."

Rook smiled. "Here's looking at you, sweetheart."

Seconds ticked by with a painful slowness. A pair of joggers rounded the corner and padded by.

Then, in his ear, Ingrid spoke up again. "The box is open. Good news, I did not explode."

"Great job!" Rook hurried back to the bench. The little metal case opened easily. Inside he found a folded piece of paper. But it was the heavy type at the top that caught his attention.

TOP SECRET—TOP SECRET—TOP-SECRET
ACCESSING THIS DOCUMENT BY UNCLEARED PERSONS IS FORBIDDEN
ON PAIN OF IMMEDIATE TERMINATION.

IF YOU HAVE FOUND THIS DOCUMENT AND DO NOT HAVE CLEARANCE,
HAND IT TO YOUR SUPERVISOR IMMEDIATELY.

SECURITY—THIS DOCUMENT IS SEC-LEVEL 6.

MAY NOT BE ACCESSED BY ANYONE WITH CLEARANCE BELOW PRIORITY 2.

Results—TASTE IMPERATIVE—Series 4200

Date: 21/04/2060
Originating: Dr. Clampen.
Confirming: M.K. Helpred, J. Mahmoud, D.S. Ingersol

test no: 4231

"We got something," said Rook, "But god knows what."

Nancy looked at the scrap of paper. "All this, for that?"

Then Ingrid spoke again. "There is more. A secondary security system has been activated. The AM-Dat file is going to explode. Please leave right now."

Rook hurled the metal case into a patch of lawn and grabbed Nancy by the arm. "Run!"

"Oh god, again?" she said.

They were about twenty feet from the park entrance when the blast wave knocked them off their feet, shattering windows all around the square. A huge London Plane tree crashed across the path, its limbs stripped and thrown across Fifth Avenue like spears. Metal crunched as a limo flipped over a pedicab.

People were screaming. Rook looked back and saw a huge cloud of gray and black smoke. He got back on his feet and helped Nancy up.

"What the fuck was in that thing?"

"Wasn't Silly Putty. Now run!"

Together they sprinted across Broadway and headed west on Twenty-third Street. By the time they'd reached the corner of Sixth Avenue the sirens had started up.

"This is turning into some day," said Nancy as they stopped to get their breath back.

The Nokia spoke up in his ear. "I have a call."

"Who?"

"Gale from the clinic."

"Put her on."

"Is this Venner?" came a voice, sounding frantic, frightened.

"Yeah."

"Somebody attacked the clinic. God, they killed everyone, I barely escaped . . . I can't believe it. They were invisible."

"Where's Plesur?"

"I didn't know what to do. She was groggy, couldn't run."

"Where is she?"

"Dead."

CHAPTER 16

"Neither of those is of any use to me." Mistress Julia waved her hand in dismissal. "That one has bruises, for god's sake."

The pimp shrugged. The pleasure model, a blond Anglo type known as a Daisy, turned away, her face closed, her eyes blank.

The sad room was full of similar pleasure models, all in the last year or so of life. There was a weariness, a deadness about them. They sat on worn plastic seats and benches, waiting to be whored out for the evening. The pleasure mods may have all started out looking exactly alike. But they certainly changed with the experience life threw at them. And these had seen the worst life had to offer.

It didn't faze Mistress Julia in the slightest. She was pitiless.

Sitting at the end of one bench was a worn-looking Pammy. Her face was lined, her eyes sunken, her golden hair had lost its sheen. Even her magnificent breasts were starting to sag. Beside her sat one of the Asian types, usually called Lotus or Blossom. She too was approaching the end of her short life, but she seemed years fresher than the Pammy.

"Come on, should be one here to meet your needs," said Frog, the heavyset pimp who ran this dump.

The green and gray carpeting was shot. The door was stained black around the edge with fingerprints. The air stank of sweat, urine, and fear. Somewhere on the fringe of consciousness, Angie wanted to turn on her heel and get the hell out of there.

The Pammy suddenly bent over and started coughing, deep, air-sucking coughs that shook her entire body. Mistress Julia looked away with a sniff. Most of the dead-end mod-bods here were sick with one thing or another.

In the last year of life their immune systems broke down. They were like flowers wilting on the vine. The best of the healthy ones got upgrades for the fight clubs.

The rest got sold to the ultimate perv market, sadists who liked to end it with a kill.

Julia could handle it.

"I specifically said virgin ass. No whip marks at all."

The pimp signaled to a dark-skinned beauty standing by herself. "Turn around, girl, and drop your panties."

Looking bored beyond life itself, the Afri-queen did as ordered, revealing a textbook gorgeous ass without a single mark.

Mistress Julia sighed. Close but no cigar. "This is nice, but not white. My player is only into white ass."

"That's all I got." Frog snapped his fingers. The Afri-queen pulled up her red silk panties and sat down.

"Did you call Rafael?"

"I'll try him again." The Frog shook his head slightly and shifted into a phone call. "Yo, dog, it's the Frog."

In the past, Julia put in her order well ahead of time and had the pleasure model delivered to her hotel in advance.

That had given her time to rehearse. The mod-bod had to
be coached, ready to give the client the cries of agony he so
desired. It had to be a real whipping, but she always used
Senforet or another topical painkiller to take the worst of
it away.

This desperate scrounging in pimp hovels for an accept-
able piece of ass was enough to make her skin crawl.

The worn-out Pammy gave a groan and pitched forward, facedown on the floor. She began twitching and
moaning, thrashing back and forth. The Blossom knelt
beside her, trying to comfort her.

Mistress Julia took a step back, but otherwise ignored
what was going on in front of her. So did the Frog, who
simply carried on making calls in search of a perfect
piece of unwhipped ass.

Angie, however, could only take so much of this. When
the Blossom started weeping, she broke down and pushed
Julia aside.

"Aren't you going to do something?"

The Frog shrugged. "I got a call out to the collection agency. They'll be 'round for the body pretty soon."

"That's it, that's all you're going to do?"

"Look, they die in here all the time. I had two die yesterday. You know the score. They're old; they only got ten years on their clock."

Angie stared at him; he turned away.

"Yeah, no marks, you got it, man."

The Pammy coughed again. "It hurt."

"What hurts?" asked Angie.

The mod-bod looked at her; the blue eyes widened, and something flickered there, unnameable, beyond the edge of life.

"Everything."

Angie saw the light go out; the blue turned dull as the head sagged back and the pleasure model died.

Her friend, the Blossom, started weeping again.

Angie felt tears welling in her eyes, but Mistress Julia had had enough. She stood up, demanding the cold, unfeeling persona that had served her so well.

The Frog gave her a big thumbs-up. "You're in luck. Fresh p-mod, no marks, young, white."

"What model?"

He grinned. "It's a Pammy, prime of life. Gonna cost you, though."

CHAPTER 17

"Plesur's gone." Rook gripped Nancy's arm, moving her into the throng of pedestrian traffic. "They found the clinic, killed everyone."

"Christ. How?"

"Must have tracked us from the taxi. We have to hide somewhere." Rook checked a street sign. They were west of the clinic now. "They'll be coming after us."

"Who the fuck are they?"

"I think it's the black ops Sangacha worked for."

They crossed Fifth Avenue and then turned north. A black van swerved to a stop ahead of them.

"Shit."

The back doors of the van flew open—but nobody got out. There was nobody inside, either.

Rook pushed Nancy through the doors of a Homebot Centre, five floors of display for new machines to run the modern home.

A handful of shoppers were watching a demonstration for a new line of machines. A device that looked like an oversized vacuum cleaner with metal arms was dusting some furniture with an attachment shaped like a very large mushroom.

The mushroom made a gentle humming noise as it polished a table while a young lady in a maroon and green uniform extolled the machine's virtues.

She looked up, annoyed, as Rook and Nancy shoved their way through the shoppers.

Irritation turned to shock as blue sparks shot from two ladies. Powerful electric shocks jolted them into the air. Panicked, people screamed and tried to run, but nobody knew which way to go. An obese lady in a red corduroy suit suddenly fell over, blocking an aisle. A display case collapsed under an invisible mass and a store security guard flew through the air, blue sparks streaming from his face and hands.

Rook ducked behind a display of electric beds, pulling Nancy down beside him.

A voice squawked over the loudspeakers: "Everyone remain calm."

It seemed a little late for that.

Rook directed Nancy past another display and hurried after her. They barreled into a room full of high-tech security systems. A security machine that looked like a lawn mower crossed with a fire hydrant patrolled, moving slowly about in a circular pattern.

The machine issued a loud whistle and announced, "Warning! You are not authorized to enter without a professional robot!"

Rook tugged Nancy b .ck, but the machine had zeroed in. It rolled up at a smart clip, illuminating them with a blast from a set of big headlights. "Remove yourself or you will be nozzled!"

From the corner of his eye, Rook caught an odd shadow wriggling like a snake along the carpet. Instinctively he ducked as something swept over his head. Arms out, he caught hold of someone in a slippery plasmonic suit. They

went down together. Rook blocked a punch with his left arm and got his right hand on the other man's face. His fingers dug into the suiting, pulling the guy toward him. The guy bucked, twisted, and heaved Rook upward in an effort to free himself. With a ripping sound, Rook fell to his left. Suddenly floating in the air was a man's face, eyes wide in consternation, mouth twisted in anger.

Rook rolled, and came up on the balls of his feet.

"You are a dead man," the assassin hissed.

"Yeah, and you're ugly," said Rook.

The eyes hardened. Rook sensed the kick, dodged

sideways. Had it connected it would have crushed his abdomen. He ducked and tried to pull out his gun but his right foot slipped on the slick floor and he went down on one knee.

Which turned out to be very lucky, because the security robot was right behind him. It unloaded a blast of patented electrified foam. Puffy goo like shaving cream shot over Rook's head. Since the puff was carrying about a thousand volts, it knocked the assassin off his feet, sparking him like a huge shrimp on a barbecue grill.

"Come on." Rook grabbed Nancy. The metal guard swiveled ominously, bringing its foam nozzle to bear on them.

Electrified foam spattered on the couch as Rook hurdled it. Nancy gave a shriek as a fleck or two hit her leg, discharging hot sparks.

They sprinted down a wide aisle between sales displays. At the end was an elevator alcove. A green light flashed and doors opened.

"Go!" Rook shoved Nancy forward.

Rook got to the elevator first, spun back, gun raised. Nancy dove past him.

He sensed someone coming fast, and stepped back into the elevator car, ready to shoot. Nancy slapped the control panel. The doors closed. But they were not alone.

Rook swung to aim at the invisible assassin, but the gun was pointed right at Nancy's chest. He flinched. Rook lost the gun as he was hammered back into the wall of the elevator. Painfully fast blows to the head, chest, and gut rained down on him. Invisible hands squeezed his throat.

He brought his arms up, trying to break the grip, and saw Nancy with the pistol in her hand, swinging with all her might. The blow landed on the back of the assassin's head, dropping him against the doors, which opened a moment later, spilling the invisible body out onto a concrete floor.

"Nice move." Rook took the gun from her as they moved quickly into the dimly lit hallway.

"Basement level, ladies lingerie, secret exits," said Nancy.

Smart-lights lit up, revealing rows of boxes and crates. They made their way to a loading dock that led back up to street level.

Rook cocked an ear. "I think they're up there, too."

"We're not going that way."

"Then where?"

Nancy pointed to a door at the rear of the loading dock. "Down."

Rook kicked in the door and they took the stairs two at a time, emerging in the boiler room. Water dripped from overhead pipes. The whole place smelled of mold and slime.

"Do you know where we're going?"

"Go deep enough, everything leads to the subway."

Rook used the Nokia to illuminate the damp space. On the far wall was an old rusty door. Rook tried it, found it was locked. He pushed Nancy back and fired a bullet into the lock.

"Jesus!" Nancy swore. "That is fucking loud!"

"Sorry." Rook pulled the door open. A dark, ominous tunnel stretched ahead.

"Interesting," said Rook.

"These tunnels link to the entire subway grid. Sometimes we use them to move mod-bods around."

A loud thump echoed above their heads.

"You want to get lost?" Nancy asked. "No place better than this."

"After you." Rook pulled the door shut behind them as Ingrid's pale blue light sliced a path in the darkness.

CHAPTER 18

"Where the hell are we?" Rook asked, wiping grime from his forehead.

Harsh mercury lights flickered over the seemingly endless subway tunnel.

"We just passed Nineteenth Street." Nancy pointed to a faded yellow and black sign. "Not much farther."

Rook felt lost in this labyrinth beneath the city, and he hated that.

Nancy had found a tunnel dug during the Emergency. From that they'd connected to the Lexington Avenue line. They now moved through the wide subway tunnel, stopping to press themselves against the walls when trains roared past.

"Here." Nancy stopped in front of a boarded-up doorway. It didn't seem very inviting. There were layers of plywood, strapped across with steel bands; the whole thing was screwed together and lacquered with adhesive.

"You got a key?" Rook studied the secure boards.

Nancy winked, then reached over and pulled a rusty lever by the track.

They waited, furtively glancing up and down the tracks for the next train.

"Nobody home?" said Rook.

Nancy hushed him, listening.

Suddenly a tiny bead of light illuminated them in red.

An irregular piece of boarding swung away, revealing a squat figure clutching an assault rifle. The man stared at Nancy, but kept the gun trained on Rook.

"Who's your friend?"

"He's a cop from upstate," Nancy answered.

The guy with the rifle tensed.

"Look, we just need somewhere to rest up for a few hours," Rook explained.

"We don't let in cops."

"This is different, believe me," Nancy insisted.

There was a long moment of silence. Rook had the feeling he was being scrutinized on camera.

The man eyed Rook. "Mr. Policeman, you armed?"

"Yes."

"Hand it over."

"Nancy told me we could trust you."

"The real question is, can we trust you?"

With a glance toward Nancy, Rook passed his sidearm to the man, who gave it to someone out of sight.

"Okay." The guard stepped back.

They entered a dark, narrow chamber. Two more figures stood nearby with rifles. A woman in black denim did the pat down and ran a chip-screen over them both.

"He's clean," she announced.

"A cop with no chips?" another guard asked, surprised.

"Long story," said Rook. "Had them pulled last night."

"Great. A rogue cop," said the first guard.

"I'm still on a case, but there's been some complications."

"Don't know, don't care."

"Thanks."

"Thank Nancy."

The man led them down a short passage. Rook noticed steel mesh netting above their heads. Another way of keeping out anyone they didn't want getting in. He'd seen it many times in the uninsured world.

"Mayor hasn't routed you guys yet?" he asked the guy with the rifle.

"Nah, that was the old days."

"Oh yeah?"

"Someone decided we're a useful safety valve down here. It's not just Eighteenth Street. There's the Deuce Hole, the Subterraneans, the Basement people, you know, and out in Brooklyn, man, we're all over the place."

Another door opened into a long space that had once been a subway station platform. Now it was a lounge filled with the denizens of the city's underworld. Low-hanging fluorescent lamps sent light rippling through the smoky haze. There were about two hundred people, perhaps more. Rook couldn't be sure, but some looked like mod-bods. A motley crowd swarmed around a bar cobbled together from pieces of steel tracks. Tables were spread up and down the platform. Men played cards as a young woman with a wild pink mohawk played guitar.

Rook grabbed two cups of coffee, and gave one to Nancy.

Sitting down, the fatigue washed over him. The morning had barely passed and it felt like he'd been going for days.

"I still can't believe Sooze is dead," Nancy sighed, then caught Rook's stare. "And the mod-bod. That was your whole case, right?"

"Yeah. Shouldn't have ended this way." Rook felt that hole in the pit of his stomach. The memory of Plesur's sunny smile, the wide, trusting blue eyes brought the anger back. Whoever was responsible for this had already destroyed his life, and now they'd taken hers.

It left him with one choice. No choice, actually.

"So what are you going to do?" Nancy asked.

"Something stupid." He picked up the Nokia. "Ingrid, you online?"

"There is a local server here."

"Get me Artoli. Secure line, if you can."

Nancy glanced at the phone. "Mind if I patch in?"

"I can manage fifty-two separate lines at once," Ingrid boasted.

A few moments later, Rook heard Lisa Artoli's voice in his ear.

"Figured it would take more than a missile to get rid of you."

Was she being sarcastic?

"They haven't stopped trying," he said.

"What about the pleasure model?"

"Dead."

"Then it's over." Artoli sounded relieved.

Rook felt wheels turning in his brain. Why was Artoli relieved to hear that Plesur was dead? He recalled what Pipo Haman had said about Sangacha's dream, that Plesur was some kind of bomb. What had Plesur known?

"Rook, get out of here," Artoli pleaded. "Go to California, that's your only chance."

"You're telling me to run?"

"Run and don't stop."

"I'm going to find out who killed her."

Artoli sighed, long and wistful. "Rook, I'm sorry."

Artoli was sorry; that was unusual. Or was he hearing something else?

Then it struck him like a hammer. Lisa Artoli had told the Feds that he had taken Plesur. She knew the Feds were going to kill him and she hadn't lifted a finger. There was guilt in her voice, that was what he was hearing.

"You gave me up," he hissed, fury boiling over.

"They were right here, they . . ." She didn't finish, but he heard the sob.

"What, put a gun to your head?"

There was a silence, then she whispered, "No. My daughter's. They were in my house. They said they would kill her."

Rook heard the fear in her voice. It was something you couldn't hide from a cop. She was telling the truth, at least to some extent.

"Jesus, Lisa. Albany can't protect you?"

"No," she said, and her voice now was very small.

Rook didn't have it in him to press her further. "Listen to me, Lisa. We've got Sable Ranch, the military, feds, probably even Washington involved. That's an awful big shitstorm over one pleasure model."

The Nokia spoke quietly in his ear. "There was an attempt to monitor the call, but I used the Taiwan Back-switch to lose it."

"Lisa, I need to ask you something."

"I have to go."

"What's the ISS?"

"The what?"

"Interservice Special Selection. Sangacha ran it."

"Shit, Rook, you'll get us both killed for sure."

Artoli cut the connection.

Rook sat there for a moment, feeling desolate. He and

Lisa went back a long way. Seemed like another life now. Going back was no longer an option, if it ever had been.

"Fuck that!" Nancy was yelling on her line. "I pay you guys plenty. You could at least tell me when something like that is coming down." She sounded pretty damned pissed off.

"No, you listen to me," she continued. "Motherfuckers in invisibility suits break into my home and try to kill me. They have a sniper team outside that kills my friend. Snipers, in broad daylight, right here in New York City! And where were the police?"

Nancy saw Rook eyeing her. She shook her head angrily.

"In other words, you aren't in charge here, in your own city!" She listened again, mouth twitching in anger. "Oh, for god's sake, Pedro, get a set of balls!"

She ended the call and turned to Rook.

"The cops say they didn't know but I don't believe them. They're afraid of something."

"Yeah, I got the same message."

"What do we do?"

"I'm open to suggestions."

Nancy chewed her lower lip. "I know someone who can give us answers."

"Is there anyone you don't know?"

"No. But this guy is not the easiest person to get to."

"Who is he?"

"The President of the United States, now retired."

Rook almost burst out laughing. "An ex-president? He'll have security all over him. We'll never get to him."

"I know a way. Used it to smuggle the girls in."

"Why did you have to smuggle them in?"

"Because we'd carry their bodies out the same way."

On Mistress Julia's first visit to the Gotham Apartments, she'd been met at the door by armed security. They'd checked her for weapons, as well as the mod-bod she'd brought to entertain her client.

She hadn't known the client's true identity and she hadn't expected the security check. She was terrified that they'd run a background check and discover she was a fugitive. But that wasn't their concern, just the weapons check and taking a visual for their internal system.

After that she'd never seen the security people again, or been asked to identify herself.

Tonight she felt the same anxiety. This time she wasn't here for the money. After the client had been satisfied, he'd often boast about his glory days of absolute power. He would offer all sorts of tantalizing things, but she'd always refused them. It had never occurred to her that he might have answers to the questions that haunted her. Who'd killed Mark? Was she a loose end that needed to be tidied up? Or had the organization been shut down? And if it wasn't—well, that information was valuable, too. Jim had convinced her of that.

Right now she needed to focus and let it happen.

Mistress Julia stalked across the marble lobby in her leather and the five-inch high heels. Over her shoulder she had a patent leather quiver with her selection of whips and crops, and behind her, shuffling submissively, was the Pammy she'd picked up from the Frog.

The mod-bod was drugged with Narcosoma, a painkiller that would take the worst off the whipping. Not that Julia could take away all of it; it was the shrieks that really got the client off.

A flunky in a red jacket and black pants nodded as she reached the elevators. Mistress Julia gave him a glare, as if she were measuring him for chains.

An older couple stood waiting for the car. They eyed her black leather and the mod-bod, crammed into a tight silk skirt and a matching blouse that showed off those luscious breasts. The woman's eyes glinted with rage as she muttered something under her breath. Mistress Julia stared back, implacable, dominant and in control. The husband, a big pink fellow in a tweed coat, kept sneaking looks at the Pammy, while trying not to let his wife see him. The couple got off at the tenth floor. The wife took her husband's hand to make sure he didn't look back at the yummy little play toy. But he did anyway.

Julia attached a leather leash to the slave collar she'd already put around the Pammy's neck. The mod-bod stared at her and mouthed something, but the Narcosoma had zonked her out.

When the doors opened on the top floor, Mistress Julia pulled the Pammy behind her and strode down the hall to the solitary penthouse apartment.

The door opened before she got there. Mistress Julia extended her right hand, on which she wore a single eight-carat faux-diamond ring. Former president Frank Marion accepted her hand and kissed the ring.

"Right on time."

"Auntie's here." Mistress Julia tugged the Pammy into Marion's apartment. "She's brought you a present."

The door closed behind them and she moved the mod-bod to the full-length mirror in the living room. The place was filled with leather furniture, antique Aubusson rugs, and paintings of cowboys pursuing cattle.

The tall, white-haired, surgically handsome ex-president came closer, smiling with bleached white teeth. "Exquisite."

"Only the best for you." Julia turned the mod-bod around, letting Marion feast his eyes on the perfect tits, ass, legs, hair, and face sculpted by genetic engineers.

"Stunning! I've never seen such a perfect specimen." President Marion ran his fingertips over the Pammy's silky smooth skin, up and down her arms, moving up to graze her neckline. His hands jumped back as if stung. "Amazing! She's ready for an earback. How did you know?"

Few things caught Julia by surprise. Locking her smile in place, she brushed aside the golden hair. Behind the Pammy's right ear, a small silver node caught the light like a diamond. A shunt. The mod had been upgraded. Only the wealthiest owners would spend that kind of money to upgrade their merchandise. Where the fuck did the Frog get this mod-bod?

Marion waved to the first shelf of the bookcase, where a display set of customized earbacks in black, white, and yellow sat like tiny glass sculptures. "I've been waiting for the perfect . . . girl to try out my new toys."

Although everyone these days used earbacks for communication and personality modifications, mods required special earbacks, not for use by humans. The most common ones artificially enhanced intelligence to a standard 120 IQ. But there were others, expensive software that altered the mod's physical systems, giving them catlike reflexes, almost superhuman strength, and god knew what else. These altered mods fought against each other in underground fight clubs with big money at stake.

"Perhaps we can work something out," Julia said coolly. "But first things first."

"Yes." Marion turned to a table where a silver champagne bucket sat with a pair of bottles sitting in the ice. Taittinger Comtes de Champagne 2056. Tall champagne flutes were set out on a tray beside it.

"To old friends," he announced, pouring for them, letting the mousse rise to the brim. He filled his own glass and joined them. "And new adventures."

The Pammy took a slow sip, wrinkled her nose in distaste, and put the glass down. Julia smiled. "Not sweet enough for some of us," she said quietly to Marion.

He smiled, nodded, obviously excited by what was going to happen.

"Pammy needs to be taught some manners." Mistress Julia downed the glass and set her quiver of whips and velvet-lined wrist cuffs on the glass table.

She checked the hook driven into the beam between the living room and the dining room. Then she swiftly cuffed the Pammy's wrists together. The baby blue eyes stared at her in a mixture of wonderment and fear. Next came the chain, which looped through an eyelet in the cuffs, and with an expert flick was tossed over the end of the hook. Mistress Julia caught the weighted end and pulled it taught.

The mod-bod's hands shot up over her head, and she cried out in sudden fear.

From the corner of her eye, Julia noted that Marion had retreated behind the golden Japanese screen, where he could see everything, but was hidden from view.

Mistress Julia quickly gagged the Pammy. Not too tight, because some screams were actually desired, but just enough

to muffle them to a bearable level. Those baby blues filled with something new, a sense of betrayal, allied to desperation and fear.

Aware that this was getting very exciting for her hidden client, she began removing the Pammy's clothing. First the top, unbuttoning and pulling it wide. The lacy bra came off in a second and the exquisite breasts spilled free. Mistress Julia rubbed her thumb over the nipples, getting them hard for her client's pleasure.

The slow sound of a zipper ripped through the still air. The mod's skirt came down and was quickly tugged free. Mistress Julia pulled hard on the back of the panties, stretching them tight over Pammy's crotch. She heard a gasp of pleasure from behind the screen.

With a sharp tug she tore the panties off, eliciting another muffled gasp.

Time to slow things down, let him get his breath back. Mistress Julia pulled on the black leather gloves, smoothing them up her arms. Then she slowly pulled out each instrument, flicking them through the air a few times before laying them on the table.

It was almost time, but Mistress Julia needed another glass of champagne. She stepped to the table and refreshed her glass, then took a sip, letting the moment build, perfectly aware of the bulging eyeballs a few feet away behind the lavish screen.

She set the glass down. In a swift motion, she smacked the rattan cane into her leather-clad palm, producing a satisfying *smack*. Spinning on her heel, she turned to the quivering, pale flesh awaiting the lash.

CHAPTER 20

When Rook and Nancy emerged at Forty-second Street, they found that the weather had changed dramatically. A sharp wind out of the east drove dark clouds across the sky, tossing trash in the air around Grand Central.

They worked their way east until they found the Gotham Apartments, a luxury building built in the 1920s with the look of a gothic mansion.

"Lights are on." Nancy pointed to the top floor. "This is our lucky night."

The Gotham building stood alone, with an office tower from the early twenty-first century at one end of the block, and a row of smaller, older buildings on the other. One of those had a coffee shop called Gotham Coffee.

"In here." Nancy led him into an alley lined with trash cans. At the back, a chain-link fence blocked off any further progress. Nancy reached through at a point where the fence was connected to the tubular steel. Rook heard a soft click and the panel of chain link slid aside as smoothly as a sliding door.

"Neat trick."

"Wait until you see the rest of this."

Behind the coffee shop, an asphalted yard connected to another building with a loading dock. In the half-light it was hard to be sure, but Rook sensed this facility hadn't seen a lot of use recently.

Nancy moved lightly up the steps to the dock, went to a door, and touched the wall beside it in two places.

A moment later it slid open.

"You got that flashlight?" asked Nancy.

He did. Inside, with the Nokia lighting the way, they stepped through an echoing, empty vault.

Rook pushed past extensive cobwebs. "How'd you find this?"

"Set up for bootleggers, early twentieth century when alcohol was illegal."

They descended a set of concrete steps, passed through another gate, and entered a wide, solidly constructed tunnel.

Nancy brushed a spiderweb. "Used to be trolleys in here, so they could deliver the whiskey under the street."

"And the security never shut it down?"

"Nope."

"Because?"

"Laws don't apply to these people."

"Doesn't make it right."

"Oh, please." Nancy sensed his disgust. "You're a rogue cop and I run a nightclub. What are we doing here?"

"No one forced you to help me." Rook grimaced. "This isn't your business."

"Sooze made it my business," she said grimly, then smiled. "I like you, SIO Venner. You risked everything for that mod."

Rook shrugged. Plesur didn't deserve her fate. "I needed her for the case."

Nancy gave him a sly smile. "If you say so."

The tunnel ended in double doors that opened easily and let them into a small subbasement.

At the far end was a narrow elevator with an open cage surrounded by brass mesh.

Rook winced as the rusted gate creaked open and Nancy stepped inside.

"You sure this thing works?"

"Last time I checked." She pulled an antique switch.

The elevator clanked as it raised them up the narrow shaft. Rook noticed the doors on each floor had been bricked up.

"Only one stop, eh?"

"That's all we need."

The elevator ground to a halt. Rook pulled back the gate and pushed on the door.

"There's a bolt," said Nancy.

Rook kicked hard at the door. It popped open immediately, slamming into something.

"Pretty flimsy really," she noticed.

He stepped out into a large kitchen with a black and white tile floor.

Nancy followed close behind. "This end of the apartment has the kitchen and the servants' quarters."

"Where are the servants?"

"They come during the day and leave in the evening."

Rook drew his sidearm, just in case.

Nancy cracked open the nearest door. "The bedrooms are down there, and beyond that there's the living room."

They came to a right turn in the corridor, and then a left. Rook heard a scream. It was a desperate sound, high and wild.

"What the fuck?" he uttered.

"Sounds like he's playing at home tonight."

The passageway widened here, floored with polished parquet. A faint smell of cologne hung in the air.

Another scream sent the hair standing up on the back of Rook's neck.

He pushed open the door and they entered a plush living room. Around the corner of the L-shaped room, a man sat behind a screen with his pants around his ankles. He was pouring himself a glass of champagne, completely oblivious to their presence. On the far side of the room, dangling from a hook, was a blond female. Standing beside her was a woman in dominatrix garb wielding a long black whip.

Cra-ack! The whip struck again. The blonde twitched and emitted a muffled scream. Rook could see she was gagged. He could also see that she was a Pammy.

Rook didn't hesitate. He stepped forward and caught the whip on the backlash, jerking it out of the dominatrix's hands.

"That's enough!"

"Who the fuck are you?" snapped the dominatrix, spinning on her high heels and glaring at him. She reached for a whip, but Nancy shoved her backward.

Rook had moved past them, focused on the Pammy. Red welts ran up and down her back and thighs.

If he didn't know better, he could swear it was Plesur. Were all Pammys truly identical—or did subtle differences change them as they lived their short lives?

He tore the gag off her mouth and unfastened the chain holding her in place. The blue eyes recognized him through the haze of pain and dope.

"Plesur?"

The irises widened, focused more tightly on him.

"Rook! You come for me." Disbelief faded into warmth and gratitude, and something else—love.

Rook shivered as he caught her with one arm and pulled her close while keeping the gun trained on the dominatrix.

"How did you get her?" he snapped.

"I bought her."

"I knew I shouldn't have trusted that bitch at the clinic!" Nancy spat.

Rook suddenly realized that he'd seen the domme's face somewhere before.

"I know you."

"You do not." The woman in black rose to her feet.

"You were there, Manuel Sangacha's place in Peekskill, when he was shot."

That staggered her. "What? I don't know what you—"

Something crashed behind the Japanese screen. Someone was struggling and cursing.

"Come join the party." Nancy stepped out from behind the screen. "Rook, may I introduce you to President Marion."

The tall figure of former president Marion stumbled behind Nancy, his face pink with anger. "Goddamn it! Don't people knock anymore?"

Rook passed Plesur to Nancy and raised the gun to cover Marion. "Don't move!"

The president shot his hands over his head. His trousers fell to the floor.

As Nancy helped the pleasure model into her skirt, Rook winced at the harsh welts on the mod's skin.

"You enjoy this line of work?" he glared at the dominatrix.

"Not particularly."

President Marion grabbed for his pants. "Do you realize how much trouble you're in?"

"You gonna send General Sangacha after me?" Rook shot back.

Marion froze, the blood draining from his face.

"What's the matter, Mr. President?" Rook taunted. "Looks like you've seen a ghost."

"If you leave now, we'll forget all about this little . . . incident," Marion said as if he were addressing his

constituents. "Take your mod with you. No harm done. She's good for plenty more of your clients."

"Shut the fuck up! I'm police, Hudson Valley Homicide, you asshole. I'm investigating the murder of General Sangacha."

Marion's mouth was working but no words came out.

The dominatrix did not like that news either. "How did you find me?"

"Why? You kill him?"

"No. I . . . provided services."

"I bet." Rook recalled the welts on Sangacha's body.

"Rook." Nancy gently turned Plesur's head to the side. Rook noticed a little ring of silver just behind her ear. So she had had the operation.

"Did it work?" he asked Nancy.

"I don't know."

"That's an expensive operation," remarked Marion. "But without the earbacks, it's useless. I happen to have quite a collection." He motioned to the array of tiny glass sculptures on the bookcase. "Take them and I'll forget you ever existed."

Rook glanced at the rack of glittering earbacks. "One of those would make her smart?"

Marion laughed. "That's not all it would do." His eyes flashed. "You know, that mod would fetch a fortune at the fight clubs."

"I can't believe I voted for you," Rook growled in disgust.

Marion favored him with a contemptuous smile.

"Look," said the leather-clad domme. "This has nothing to do with me." She started gathering her things.

"No one goes anywhere!" Rook instructed. He turned to Marion. "Why was Sangacha killed?"

"You can't expect me to answer that."

Rook advanced threateningly. "Let's try again." He slid the safety off. "What the fuck is going on?"

"I'm an *ex*-president. Why would they tell me?"

"Who? The Ranch?"

Panic flashed across Marion's eyes. "You really don't want to get involved with this."

"No shit. Someone killed Sangacha and has been trying to kill me and the Pammy. Why?"

Marion shook his head. "Manuel Sangacha had many enemies. I have no idea how the mod fits in."

"She belonged to Sangacha."

"Fuck!" the dominatrix exclaimed.

Rook glanced at her. "You got something else to say?"

The mistress glared back, her eyes cold as ice. "This is all a mistake."

"Yeah, you said it."

Rook fished in his pocket and brought out the ISS badge. "Recognize this, Mr. President?"

Marion flinched as if he'd been slapped in the face. He strode to the table and poured himself a glass of champagne. "Where the hell did you get that?"

"Sangacha's apartment."

Marion swigged the rare vintage like it was beer. "This great nation went through a crisis, I'm sure you understand that much."

"The Emergency," Rook said.

"Things got messy."

"So they used Sangacha and the ISS to clean things up." Rook held up the badge. "We're talking about a government-run death squad."

"That's a crude way to put it."

Rook gestured to the dominatrix. "Sangacha had so many fucking nightmares, he had you come over and beat the shit out of him."

The dominatrix stared in shock. "They were after the mod, not me."

"Yeah, we're all real lucky," Rook shot back. "Is the ISS still operational?" he asked Marion.

"You'd have to ask the Ranch."

"I can arrest you right now for conspiracy, Mr. President."

Marion laughed. "Detective, get serious. This is all hearsay. You got nothing. Nothing!"

Rook pulled out the paper he'd taken from the metal file. "What's Taste Imperative?"

Marion gave a strangled shriek and staggered to his feet, champagne glass crashing to the floor. "Don't say another word!"

Rook stared at him. "What's wrong with you?"

Marion waved his hands frantically. "You don't know what you're doing. Please, I beg you!"

"What is Taste Imperative?"

"No. I can't!" Marion screamed. "Don't! Don't even think those words . . ."

With a heavy wet thud, like a hammer smashing a watermelon, Marion's head exploded.

CHAPTER 21

"Get down!" Rook dove to the floor as Marion's corpse toppled backward. The legs twitched twice, then went still.

Rook looked around wildly. Had there been a sniper? Was someone in the room?

But no shots followed. He heard someone vomiting and saw Nancy huddled in a corner.

"Jesus Christ!" The dominatrix was on her knees, hands over her mouth, staring with bulging eyes at the ruin of the ex-president of the United States. Blood and brains stained her glossy boots.

Rook crawled to the window. Wind buffeted the glass, but there were no bullet holes. He slowly got to his feet, aware of the gore dripping down his shirt.

"What the hell did you do, Rook?" muttered Nancy.

Rook shook a piece of flesh off the paper he'd retrieved from the explosive file.

"I just asked him about this."

"And his fucking head exploded!"

"Was he shot?" asked the domme.

"No," said Rook. "He must have had an explosive chip in his head."

Nancy wiped at the gristle on her clothes. "That is some fucked up shit."

"The technology's not new." Rook carefully edged toward the window and scanned the street, checking the other buildings, as well. It was raining hard now. "We use them on a felon's ankle. If he moves out of range or tampers with it, it explodes and takes his leg."

"Jesus."

"Cheaper than jail."

Nancy shook her head. "What could be so important they'd blow President Marion's head off?"

"Same reason they tried to blow our heads off." Rook moved to check on Plesur. "Her." The mod lay on the couch, eyes shut. "She's the key. And one thing's for sure.

Whoever killed the president is sending over the cleanup squad."

Nancy scanned the apartment. "We need some clothes."

The domme pointed down the hall. "There's a wardrobe in the bedroom."

Nancy padded to the room, removing her shirt.

The dominatrix shoved her equipment into a bag and glanced at Rook. "She didn't feel all the pain. Just enough so she'd scream."

"Beating someone who wants it is one thing," growled Rook.

Her eyes met his. "I needed to get to him." She gestured at the headless body. "Look, I was there at Sangacha's when they killed him. I barely escaped."

"Why didn't you report it?"

The blond leather-clad woman laughed. "You're joking, right?"

PLEASURE MODEL

Rook did not look as if he was joking.

"I thought the killers were after me." She straightened up. "Now I'm *totally* fucked."

"Two clients die on you, might be time for a new job." Nancy returned with an armful of clothes. She tossed a clean blue shirt and a pair of khakis at Rook. "But you did bring us the mod. We owe you for that."

Rook nodded, wadding the clothes into a ball. "Change outside. Don't leave anything here."

"She's waking up." Nancy helped Plesur to her feet. Her head lolled to one side, golden hair spilling across her face.

"Let's move." Rook jammed a fresh ammo clip in his gun.

They started back toward the kitchen, heading for the bootlegger's elevator.

With a terrifying boom, the apartment's front door blew open as dark-suited figures rushed in.

"Nobody move!" bellowed a deep voice.

"You, down on the floor!" A man shoved Rook roughly.

Rook raised his hands slowly, and dropped to his knees as a man in full tac suit pointed an M-25 at him.

"Confirmed. The president is dead," said a voice.

Tac-radios squawked softly among the heavily armored men.

"Get the body bag in here now!" said another voice.

Rook noticed Plesur leaning against Nancy, their backs against the wall. Nancy was adjusting something behind Plesur's right ear. Then one of the tac-team motioned to them with his weapon.

"Down on the floor. Now!" he barked.

"You don't want to do this," Rook called out. "I'm a police officer."

"Shut up!" The man jammed the M-25 against Rook's head. "Bring the mod, kill the others."

How the hell did they know about Plesur?

The world suddenly turned upside down as something knocked the heavy gun away.

Plesur came off the wall so quickly she was a blur. Rook had never seen a human being move so fast. The guy in front of her went flying through the air with a kick to the stomach, his automatic weapon now in her hands. With blue sparks and a sharp crack, the gun sprayed bullets.

Two members of the tac-squad went down firing wildly.

Rook rolled himself flat on the floor, pulling Julia down. He looked up, saw Nancy stagger as bullets ripped through her in quick succession. She crashed over a table and fell by Rook's side. She grasped his hand, shuddered, and was gone.

Plesur cartwheeled behind a sofa and came up to a vertical position, firing off the whole clip. Three more men went down. Vaulting the sofa, she tossed the commander into the wall, then spun around to shoot the last member of the tac-squad right through the faceplate.

He hit the floor, and there was silence.

The wind suddenly rattled the windows as lightning flashed over the city.

Rook and Julia struggled back to their feet.

"My god!" exclaimed Julia.

"God had nothing to do with it." Rook opened his fist. Nancy had deposited the rest of the earbacks into his hand.

He stood up and faced the killing machine that was Plesur. She studied him through steel-glinted baby blues.

Rook slowly touched her face. "That was really some-thing."

Plesur suddenly focused on Mistress Julia. Her left hand whipped out faster than the eye could follow.

Before Rook could say a word, Plesur backhanded Julia across the face. The domme spun backward, crum-pling to the floor.

"I heard they get angry," Julia muttered. There was a vivid red line down one side of her face.

"How do you feel?" Rook asked. Plesur looked at him, her eyes uncertain.

"I know some things, but not others. It is strange."

"You really helped."

The mod faced him, shoulders back, head held high. "I help Plesur now."

"Welcome to the world." He covered Nancy's face with a tablecloth. "The good and the bad."

Julia got to her feet, rubbing her jaw. "If your pleasure mod hadn't gone psycho, we'd all be lying right alongside her."

"Yeah," Rook said dryly, depositing the earbacks in his pocket.

Plesur tossed each of them a raincoat from the closet.

"More like them will come," she announced.

"Where can we go?" Julia asked.

Plesur stopped to think. "74 17 06 97 57 87 56 61."

Rook stopped in his tracks. "What was that?"

"In my head. I am supposed to remember it."

Rook held Plesur's arms, studying her face. "A number?"

"I just remembered."

"What is that?" Julia asked.

Rook pulled out the Nokia. "Ingrid, you catch that?"

"Geographical coordinates," the phone answered. "A location eighty-six miles from here."

Rook felt his heart jump as he slung an M-25 over his shoulder. "I love my phone."

"Thank you," Ingrid buzzed.

Plesur cocked the M-25 and slipped three ammo clips in the waistband of her skirt. "We must go."

"You still want some answers?" Rook asked Julia as they rushed through the kitchen.

"Yes." Julia slipped into the elevator.

"You might just get them."

Outside the rain was hammering down and the wind was gusting fiercely.

"Who are you?" Rook asked the domme.

The woman in leather hesitated, as if debating the answer to the question.

"Just call me Julia." She pulled her coat tight around her. "And who the fuck are you, some supercop?"

"Yes." Plesur smiled. "And a good man."

Turning her face to the rain, gun ready, the ex-pleasure mod led the fugitives into the storm.